GANGSTRESS
COLLECTION

BRANDON McCALLA

spot
rushers

THE NOVELLA
BOOK ONE

AUGUSTUS
PUBLISHING

This is a work of fiction. Names, characters, places, and incidents are products of the author's imagination or are used fictitiously and are not to be construed as real. Any resemblance to actual events, locales or organizations, or persons, living or dead is entirely coincidental.

Copyright 2007 Brandon McCalla
ISBN: 0979281628

Edited by Anthony Whyte
Design: Sublime Visuals
Photography: Jason Claiborne & Sanyi Gomez

All rights reserved. No parts of this book may be used or reproduced in any manner whatsoever without written permission, except in the case of brief quotations embodied in critical articles and reviews. For further information contact Augustus Publishing

First printing Augustus Publishing paperback October 2007

AUGUSTUS PUBLISHING
AugustusPublishing.com
info@augustuspublishng.com

BRANDON McCALLA

This book ain't for punks!
This for my gangsta women, those who stood by me in my Hip Hop fiction struggle. I write in so many different genres and have positioned myself at times more distinctively than this fiction world deserves. Most don't care about diversity or the difference, me I try to make a difference and appreciate diversity.

This book is for the ladies who stood by me in this. This is for Deesha Latoya my special vixen from St. Louis, for Yanta my west coast shorty and for my southern peer the author Danielle Santiago. This is for my forever publicist Nakea Murray, for Virgo, who has always put up a good fight and for Quana, the dame who got most of the manuscripts I've written when they were but a fetus.

This is for Sonia the woman who definitely would ride or die for me if I was riding and prepared to die, this is for my peer and fellow author Kashan who is gangsta enough to curse me out,

hang up on me and call me right back just to curse me out and hang up again, and this is for Kim because I went to see her in the hospital and she recovered real quick because she's a strong bitch. I use the word bitch loosely but only in jest and for fun. None of you are bitch's, you are all lovely black women, beautiful women with beautiful minds.

What up Vickie Stringer, Noire, Anna J, Carla Dean, the ever so lovely Nneka, Theresa, my best friend Danni (I love you), Denise Campbell (I see you), Juwania, Natasha my book mistress, Lenaise Williams (stop doing nasty stuff on the cam!), KaShamba Williams!!!, my MOMS!!!, Monique Patterson!!!, Candace Cottrell, Delonya, Azarel!!!, Brenda Thomas, Dawn (Philly), and Tanya Nunez.

We got Vashni and Vee and all the lovely ladies all over the world in Borders and Walden's book stores, and every Barnes n Nobles with an urban book section and a hot looking cashier, what up!

What up Milky! Let me shout out my cousin Wendy from Harrisburg Pennsylvania real quick. Deborah Smith!!!, Puerto Rican and journalistically wise and sexy Jackie (I'm gonna call you), my nieces Jade and Dorothy, Glamour and Crystal (C2C), Maxine, the beautiful Robyn Moffett (keep singing), the Queen of all media Wendy Williams!!!, Ericka, Frances, Seiko, Doreen, Sabrina, Olivia and Lorna!!!, Samantha, Zenobia, Audra, Angel, Shannon, Meisha (rep Brooklyn), BLUNT !!!(Kimberly), Shamora Lowe!!!, Shawnda

Grundy (where are you Sha?), and my buddy Sherella.

I didn't forget about T.N. Baker, and my girl Tessa and Summer and Xanyell. I see you Tu!!! (Ex factor), Hadiya!!!, and Jazzie (where art thou Jazzie?), Karen Miller!!!

Nards Baby!!!

...Baby Girl (yeah you!), Chase (thank you for being a good reader), Rain (congradulations!!!), and Troublesome (stay in school!!!), and Trina (Intellectual's), to every jump-off and pop-off who momentarily relieved my stress (you are appreciated)...

Nikki Turner, what up, woman? Venetia Ward learn what patience and loyalty is and to the fans because I'm a fan of the fans. I love your fingers because they turn the pages of the book and keep turning them till there ain't any pages left.

I ain't miss nobody because all of you are inside my head, thus if I didn't mention you I'm thinking about you nonetheless, never doubt. I love all of you, the book clubs, C2C, Rawsistas, the Mahogany book club, As the page turns, everyone who blogs on to www.literaryhood.blogspot.com

PROLOGUE

The year was 1999. They left Brooklyn, New York at 11 o'clock at night, traveled for three hours reaching the south west side of Philadelphia Pennsylvania around 2 o'clock in the morning. Sabrina drove the red Ford Taurus, Dora Dean rode shotgun while Rayne and Bernadette were in the backseats. They had spent the trip joking around, listening to rap music and smoking weed. They piped down and got serious when they arrived at their destination.

Dora Dean crouched low in her seat. Her feet were resting on the dashboard. She kept nodding off during the trip. Now Dora was wide awake and ready for whatever.

Bernadette took the clip out of her gun and slapped it back in. She loved the sound loading a gun made.

Rayne rolled up one leg of her pant and touched the handle of her .22 automatic pistol nestled in the ankle holster. It was her secondary weapon. She didn't have a gun fetish like the rest of them. Rayne favored the long machete blade sitting on her lap. She preferred cutting and slicing above anything else.

They slowly drove by the house and parked right across the street. Sabrina looked at Dora Dean and said, "This hood looks all quiet and shit, ain't nobody outside. What sort of hood is this?"

"What sort of hood do you want it to be bitch? You want a hood full of witnesses?" Dora snapped.

"You got the key?" Sabrina asked.

"What the fuck you think, I left that shit back in Brooklyn?" Dora asked reaching into her coat pocket and producing the key. "We fucked. He fell asleep. I got the front door key and went to the hardware store and made a copy, just like you told me to," Dora said smiling at Sabrina. "This shit's gonna be easy. What's the matter?"

Rayne laughed. Sabrina turned around and gave Rayne a ferocious stare. Rayne's laughter ceased.

"I ain't scared, bitch. I'm just smart enough to be careful," Sabrina said turning the lights off. She left the engine running and looked at the passengers in the backseats. "This is it. We're gonna open the front door and soldier inside. If anyone's home or tries to get gangsta, let em eat lead." She looked over at Dora. "You said he keeps the money in a box that he stashes up under the kitchen sink?"

"Yup…"

"Does he roll with many nigga?" Sabrina questioned.

"A lot of niggas and he holding a lot of money," Dora smiled. "I told y'all we might have problems tonight. There might be three...four niggas with straps up in there. It'll be worth it. That nigga be doing it. And a whole lot of money is under his sink."

Bernadette spoke with a coarse voice. "I know we went over this already but remember as soon as we go inside, me and Dora are gonna head straight to the kitchen. Sabrina you keep 'em niggas steady if they around. Anyone acts the fool...you start shooting."

"It ain't like it won't be the first time we killed some fucking fool," Rayne said to Sabrina. She reached under the seat for a double-barreled shotgun.

"Give me my Dick," Sabrina said when she saw it.

Rayne handed her the shotgun and chuckled.

A man and woman were walking down the sidewalk across the street. Sabrina eyed them cautiously until they were out of sight.

"Rayne you stay in the car. We might have to run out so please keep your eyes on the door."

"Humph..." Rayne huffed and pouted.

She didn't want to be the getaway driver again. Rayne took immense pleasure from the violence. Dora was the best driver but she also knew the lay out of the crack house. Rayne didn't. Rayne knew it made perfect sense for her to be the getaway driver.

With her broad shoulders, Bernadette was the biggest out of all of the girls. She was a husky looking mean bitch. The dude always have them rowdy type niggas with him. If things got out of hand, she'd become very necessary. Sabrina wasn't a good driver. Her skills were in her gun use. She wouldn't hesitate blasting anyone.

"Leave your doors open bitches," Rayne said.

"Good idea," Sabrina said pulling the ski mask all the way over her face.

Bernadette had a bandanna tied around the lower part of her face; revealing only her eyes. Her hair was cut short like a man. Dora pushed her hair back with a hand and then pulled a stocking down over her head.

Sabrina check the shotgun in her hand, her Dick was erect and ready to bust off. Bernadette slapped the clip in the 9mm one last time, just to hear the sound of it. Dora pulled out her weapon, a 32. The three inched toward the house.

It was early Saturday morning and winter. Few people hung outside in the cold. They were in the hood, the south west side of Philly, Sabrina felt things were too quiet. She figured someone was around and they just didn't see them. It didn't matter, this spot was gonna be rushed regardless.

"Okay bitches, let's do the damn thing."

one

Rayne saw the way Sabrina was backing out of the house and immediately knew something was wrong. It was all in the way she was moving. Sabrina was staggering backwards and trying to reload her shotgun.

Rayne heard gunshots coming from inside the house from across the street. She was about to hop right out the car and run in with her machete and pistol but had to stick with the plan. She was supposed to wait until they were all out of the house.

Rayne saw Sabrina clutching her stomach and falling. Sabrina had been shot. Rayne opened the door and ran across the street. Bernadette was shooting at someone on the other side as she backed out the house.

"We gotta get out of here," she yelled. "Dora's dead."

"What...?" Rayne shouted in exasperation. She clutched the machete and gun, confusion registered on her face.

There was a glass-shattering explosion. One of the windows at the front of the house blew up. Bullets from a big gun rained out the window leaving Bernadette wet. Rayne screamed. She purposely dropped the machete while running towards the house. Clutching her .22 with both hands, Rayne fired in the direction of the window. Shots came back at Rayne. She dived down and hit the concrete. She scraped her hands badly and lost her gun.

Sabrina ran to where Rayne was and knelt over her. Rayne saw the blood all over Sabrina. Most of it leaked from a hole around her stomach. The wound looked wicked.

"Dora is dead," Sabrina said in a weak voice.

Rayne froze, caught up in disbelief. Bernadette had gotten shot right in front of her eyes. She grabbed Sabrina's shotgun then started crawling across the front lawn closer to Bernadette. She watched in horror as another bullet tore though Bernadette's left leg. Rayne quickly jumped up from crawling and began running to her.

Finally she was at the front of the action, her hands bloody and sweating.

The man shooting from the window made his way to the front door. Rayne wasn't sure if Sabrina's shotty was loaded or not but as soon as he came outside, Rayne let the shotgun rock.

It was pure luck, Sabrina had reloaded.

Her first shot missed dude, tearing off a portion of the door. He hesitated. Rayne let off another round before he could shoot. The bullet ripped through his chest. It blew a portion of his spine and whatever was inside his stomach out the other side of him.

Rayne saw red, nothing but blood. She wasn't sure what to do next. Dora was dead but she didn't want to believe it. She would go in the house and find her.

"Dora ain't dead…!" She yelled.

"Help me…" Rayne heard Bernadette's feeble cry.

Rayne was close to her. She looked at her friend and shuddered. Bernadette's condition seemed to be worse than Sabrina.

"I'm here," Rayne said walking to her friend and kneeling down. She examined Bernadette and saw numerous bullet wounds.

Rayne dropped the shotgun. Bernadette was big and tall, but Rayne managed to help her up. They tottered in the dark back to where Rayne had left Sabrina. She wasn't there.

A bright light hit Rayne directly in the face. She wanted to raise a hand to her face but couldn't. Bernadette could barely walk and she didn't dare let her go. Rayne wasn't going to be able to keep this up much longer.

The bright light came from the Taurus. Sabrina was driving

and rolled to a stop. Rayne helped Bernadette into the backseat then she hopped into the passenger seat and closed the door. Sabrina was leaning with her head all the way back on the neck rest. Her eyes were closed, blood poured out of her.

Rayne didn't care who was in the house or if they'd come out shooting. Dora was dead. Rayne couldn't stand to see anymore of her friends killed. She hopped out the car and ran to the driver's side. Rayne pushed Sabrina with all of her strength onto the passenger seat. She gunned the car forward not caring where she was going.

"What the fuck happened?" Rayne yelled. She jerked the steering wheel maneuvering out of the way of another speeding car. Rayne was driving on the opposite side of the road and may have collided with an oncoming vehicle if it wasn't early morn.

"What the fuck happened?" She repeated.

"We fucked up big-time." Bernadette said between pangs of pain searing through her. "Dora's dead," she managed to grunt before closing her eyes.

"Fuck!" Rayne yelled.

She didn't know what to do or where to go. Rayne was driving on the opposite side of the road and decided to get on the right side. The car shook as it hit the divider in the road. Rayne remained in control.

"You gotta find a hospital," Bernadette worded to Rayne.

Rayne glanced over at Sabrina. She appeared as if she

was still breathing. She was way too scared to find out.

"Can you check on Sabrina?" She asked Bernadette.

Bernadette grimaced, moved closer and grabbed Sabrina roughly by the hair. Sabrina moaned.

"The bitch's alive," Bernadette announced. Bernadette didn't have feeling in her left leg anymore, but the bullet in her back was hurting like hell.

"Find a hospital, Rayne," Bernadette yelled.

"I ain't never been here before. I don't know where nothing is," Rayne shot back.

A few minutes later, she spotted a road sign. They weren't far from a hospital. Luck was on their side.

"Thank God…" Rayne sighed.

She drove the car to the hospital's emergency area, hit the back of a parked EMS truck. Rayne stumbled out of the car. She saw one of the hospital's security guards. He saw Rayne, the blood on the car and instantly knew that something was wrong.

"Help us please!" Rayne yelled.

She grabbed him by his shirt, clutched him until he forcefully pried her hands away.

"My friends are inside the car." She yelled. "They've been shot."

two

Rayne raised her head up off the table. The detective came back into the room carrying a cup of coffee and a pack of cigarettes. The items had been requested by Rayne.

Her emotions were running like a faucet and her nerves were electrified like lightning. She was shaking uncontrollably and had no control of herself. Everything was crumbling down right in front of her. Rayne needed her medication. She virtually had no idea of where she was. Her mind needed stabilization. Rayne could've sworn she was just inside a cell. Rayne didn't have a clear mind but she remembered someone asking if she wanted something, she told them coffee and cigarettes.

Rayne wasn't sure if Sabrina and Bernadette were alive or dead. The authorities had taken her into custody for questioning

a couple hours after she arrived at the hospital. They found guns in the Taurus and put her under arrest. Now she was in desperate need of her medication.

Rayne was handcuffed and fingerprinted. They ran her name through the computer. She was then placed in a cell where she lost her mind and couldn't focus on anything. She couldn't stand this anymore. She needed her medication and drifted off into a deep sleep. When Rayne woke up she was in an indiscrete room with an officer behind her. She was in cuffs. Rayne didn't even remember getting roused from sleep or how she'd gotten out of the cell.

The officer removed the cuffs and told her to sit at a table where there were two chairs on each side. Rayne was cuffed to the chair and the officer walked out. Rayne looked around not knowing whether things were happening the way she remembered them. She was still looking through eyes that saw only red, eyes that saw blood. Time was jumbled.

"My name is detective Charles Burrows," He said once he walked into the room. Rayne stared blankly at him. He was black and close-to-middle-age. "Do you want anything?" He asked.

"I wanna be let out of here," Rayne said looking mystified.

The detective appeared amused, he laughed.

"How about some coffee and cigarettes." Rayne blurted at him.

He walked out the room without another word. Came back in with what she wanted and sat down in the other chair. Rayne had finally put things together. Her eyes were leaking tears that just wouldn't stop coming down. She reached for the pack of cigarettes with a shaking hand. Rayne saw a book of matches on the table and an ashtray. She moved the ashtray closer to her.

For Rayne things were moving in slow motion, it was like she was living in a horror flick, a nightmare. She was having problems striking the match. The detective didn't even notice her difficulties.

"Help me get this shit lit you fuck!" Rayne shouted.

"Feisty..." The detective laughed. Instead of striking the match he took the cuff off of her shackled hand.

"Thanks," she deadpanned.

After a couple of tries, Rayne lit the cigarette and took a long drag. She exhaled then broke down crying dejectedly. Detective Charles Burrows watched her with a curious expression. She looked up at him.

"What the fuck...? Say something you fuck!"

"Dora Dean Watson is dead. Shot two times in the back of her head." Charles Burrows spoke slowly counting his words. He looked directly as he continued. "The forensic on the scene said she seemed to have been engaged in some sort of fight or struggle that left her with some initial head trauma before the execution."

"Execution...?" Rayne repeated. She was bewildered.

"Not an execution, huh...? You tell me what it was then. Your friend Dora was beaten unconscious then shot. What were you girls doing on the south side of Philly? You are a long way from New York City. The house Dora's body was found in is a well known crack house. Two other women were shot. There was a man's body found inside the house, dead from a slug from a shotgun found twenty feet from the house and another man inside the house without a head, dead from a slug from that very shotgun."

"So...?" Rayne asked.

She took another puff from the cigarette, rested it in the ashtray and wiped her tears. They all wore gloves. During the drive, when Rayne was searching for a hospital she made Bernadette collect the gloves and toss them out the window. Rayne thought about Sabrina and Bernadette, She started crying again.

"My girls, are they okay?" Rayne's voice was strained with concern.

"Alive yes," Charles Burrows laughed. "None of you are okay. You're all in deep shit, deep trouble. You best tell me, what were you all doing at the house. Don't make it harder on yourself."

"What makes you think we were there?"

"How about blood samples that match Sabrina's and Bernadette's...?"

The detective stood up and moved his face closer to

Rayne's.

"Do you know how much time has gone by since you've been in custody? No you don't. You were pretty messed up, not like your friends but emotionally and mentally. We pulled your records, had to get them from New York. You are highly anemic. You're bipolar with a manic depressive personality. Rayne, you're a real piece of work. We were able to get you your medication, Lithium, Zoloft, iron pills. The medical record suggested we get them and get them fast. It seems you're some type of a lunatic." The detective laughed.

"Fuck you!" Rayne shouted.

The detective became serious and stared at her.

"Read me my fucking rights." She shouted even louder.

"You were in such an emotional state we weren't able to get anything but rambling out of you. It's Monday morning. You don't even remember your stay in the cell, now do you?"

Rayne straightened her back. The detective's words had stunned her. She sat quiet, almost pensive.

"Fuck you!" Rayne rose from the chair, grabbed it and tossed it at the detective.

He ducked narrowly evading the chair. The detective became enraged and flipped the table over. Rayne backed away from him, scanning the room for anything she could use as a weapon. Before she could react, the detective grabbed her by the hair and forced her against the wall. He got real close to her. His

massive body pinned Rayne's five foot-six inch, one hundred and twenty pound frame to the wall. She was an extraordinary mixture of Puerto Rican and Black, her hair was long.

"Get off...you dirty ass, motherfucking freak..."

Obscenities were hurled at him but the detective kept his fingers tangled up in her tress. Her breathing went shallow as he thrust her face into the wall.

Rayne felt what could've been his erection poking her ass while he held her. He smashed his body up against hers, flattening her against the wall. Her breasts were hurting and her breathing was labored.

"You are gonna go to jail for a long time Rayne Avila," he hissed in her ear. "Your girls are talking. All of you are going to jail."

She smelt the detective's nasty breath. She wanted to scream but didn't want to give him anymore pleasure.

"If you wanna make it easier, you better tell me something good."

It was definitely his dick. The detective was grinding his midsection into her while he had her hemmed up. She felt him get harder against her ass.

"You nasty ass, motherfucka..."

She felt her airflow cut-off. Rayne could barely get the words out. The detective loosened his hold on her hair and grabbed her by the neck. He threw her to the floor. Rayne stared at him with indifference. She could only see red. The detective composed himself and put the table back on its legs.

"Sit down." Detective Burrows ordered. "And you best tell me what happened on Saturday morning? Tell me why you were at Steve Sanford's crack house and why Dora Dean Watson's body was found on the kitchen floor battered and bruised with two bullets to the back of the head."

"I don't fucking know," Rayne said then started crying again. "Put me back in the fucking cell. I don't know shit and I ain't telling you nothing."

"You ain't telling, but your girls are. They are chirping like canaries."

Rayne gave a hysterical shriek. "I'm fucking crazy!"

"You're going to jail too. Whether you say shit or not, you're all going to jail. We got enough to lock you, Sabrina and Bernadette up but Dora, she's dead. Don't you care about her?"

"Fuck you!" Rayne shouted.

She jumped out of her seat. So did the detective. They were both standing on opposite sides of the table staring at each other. Rayne had tears in her eyes. Detective Burrows began laughing again.

"You need to take your medication," he said.

"I need to speak to my lawyer."

"What lawyer? You'll get your time in court and you'll get one appointed to you. Nothing you say, nothing a lawyer says is

gonna help you or bring Dora back to life. You girls fucked up. You know you fucked up right? This isn't the first time you've done this, it's just the first time shit got fucked up."

"Done what?" Rayne snapped. "Just what did we do?" Rayne began the hysterical laughter again. "I want my meds, You know. I'm fucking crazy!"

three

She was locked inside the cell. An hour later an officer handed her two pills, a bottle of water and a sandwich between the bars. Rayne took everything. She squat back down on the only piece of furniture in the cell, a hard bench. Rayne swallowed the pills after downing the ham and cheese sandwich. Then she lay back on the bench.

Her mind began to slowly adjust itself. She hated the way the medication made her feel. It left her far too relaxed and too weak. But without it she wasn't able to function normally. Her skin crawled when she thought of the violence outside the house. Rayne wished she had gone inside. Rayne laughed at the thrill of the violence. The medication stopped her from shaking. That was the best thing about taking it.

She yawned.

"Dora," She uttered her friend's name. "Dora, they got you girl. You were my bitch. Sabrina, Bernadette, you're all my bitches."

Dora wasn't the one she was the closest to, Sabrina was. They had shared everything, including the same man.

Rayne thoughts flowed back to when she first met Sabrina. It was like the planets were aligned that day.

She let out a laugh. "Who would've thought shit would go down like this. Dora baby, they got you."

Rayne was known for talking to herself for hours but she was in the belly of the beast, where she had to keep her mouth shut. Her shit had to stay tight. She was fucked up, in jail. Where did it begin? Rayne wondered.

It was beyond what happened Saturday night, beyond the drug dealer, Steve Stunner and the box full of money under the kitchen sink in the crack house. It started with the bond she had with her girls. The four of them together were called the Fatal Four. They were spot rushers they robbed drug dealers. It was what they did. That was how they earned their living.

Trevor had named them the Fatal Four. He had set things in motion. Rayne smiled. Thoughts of Trevor overwhelmed her. She missed him inside her. Trevor was the only man she'd ever let shoot sperm up in her.

Trevor had to die. Love for her girls went beyond even

the nigga who helped form the union. Rayne thought about her girl Sabrina. Sabrina killed Trevor. Trevor didn't deserve to die. He was fucked up but so were the others. None of them were anything nice but they had fun times.

The wheels of Rayne's mind kept spinning back in time. She thought back to how tall Sabrina looked when she'd first seen her. Sabrina looked like an Amazon in the hood. She was five feet eleven and weighed about a hundred and sixty pounds. She was a healthy looking girl, not husky and manly looking like Bernadette. Sabrina was beautiful. She had the prettiest face.

Trevor was Sabrina's man first. Sabrina had found out about Rayne and threatened to beat her ass. Sabrina was always out in the streets fighting some bitch. It didn't matter the size of these girls, Sabrina beat their asses all the same.

Sabrina had told Rayne that she used to study karate and ballet when she was younger. She was from good upbringing unlike Rayne, who came from shit. Rayne was born and raised in the Bronx. She came from the sperm of a dope-fiend and was birthed from the womb of an alcoholic.

Everyone who was around to see Sabrina and Rayne square off, knew it would be a good fight. Rayne wasn't very big. Back in '94 she was a skinny thing. She'd gain weight later. Rayne wasn't a punk. She was part of the streets like asphalt was part of the blacktop. She was out everyday selling drugs with Trevor, her man and Sabrina's.

It was the middle of the day. Sabrina popped up on the corner where Trevor plied his trade. Rayne was there all up under his ass. There was no hesitation, Sabrina ran up on her, grabbed her long hair and repeatedly swung at her face. Rayne was hit about a dozen times before she was able to reach up and scratch Sabrina's eyes.

Rayne heard the scream and knew she damaged Sabrina's once undamaged face. Rayne went in for the kill and was punching Sabrina's face. Sabrina delivered a kick that seemed straight out of a Kung Fu flick.

Rayne went down to her knees clutching her midsection. Sabrina didn't stop. She was on her like a cheap suit, jumping on top with punches raining upside Rayne's head. Sabrina beat Rayne until her nose was bloody. Trevor was able to pull Sabrina off a defeated and temporary disabled Rayne. Sabrina turned her anger on Trevor and started fighting him.

He wasn't for bitches hitting him. Trevor had a rep to protect. He smothered Sabrina's punches. She kept coming and finally he smacked her in the face. Sabrina was tall but Trevor was taller. Sabrina was crying, angry, wanted to kill Trevor but she loved him. So did Rayne.

They were both eighteen years old. Rayne had been out on her own since she was fifteen years old. She wasn't safe in her house. Her father was the sort of man who used to sexually assault his own children. Neither friends nor cousins were exempt from his indiscretions. Rayne's mother was so drunk; most of the time she didn't even know what day it was. Rayne was sick and tired of her father's ways so she ran away from home.

Sabrina was raised in an upper middle class community in Brooklyn and had gone to catholic school. Besides being beautiful, she was spoiled and a bad ass. She was a sucker for peer pressure. Her father was a foreman at a small construction company. He died in a fluke accident on the job when Sabrina was only fourteen. After that, her mother seemed to care less and less about anything. Then along came Trevor and Sabrina went big for him. His mother lived a couple of blocks from Sabrina.

They started a relationship when she was fifteen. His affair with Rayne started when she was sixteen. They both weren't gonna give him up without a fight.

Blood was all over Rayne's tank top. She spat a razor out of her mouth and into her right hand. Trevor saw and knew Rayne was crazy. They lived together and he always made sure she took her medications.

"You better bounce," Trevor said to Sabrina as Rayne staggered up with the blade.

Sabrina didn't budge and caught a buck-fifty on her beautiful face. The thin slice started from the lower part of her left eye and ended at the bottom of her jaw. A second later blood was all over the place. Rayne just remembered all the red. Whenever things turned violent she'd go blank and all she saw was crimson,

blood dripping. Sabrina stayed and fought despite the cut. Trevor held Sabrina back. Rayne swung the razor again but missed.

When Rayne spat blade it always turned into something awful. She was kicked out of high school for carving up another student. The girl came out of the hospital with over two hundred stitches on her face. The poor girl looked like Edward Scissorhands.

Rayne went overboard with everything. She was an extremist when she wasn't on her meds. The day she was introduced to Sabrina, Trevor made sure she had taken her medication. He felt responsible for her and kept her fed three times a day. Rayne never had any sort of appetite, she was anemic.

It all came to an end when Sabrina murdered Trevor. The vision replayed in Rayne's mind like it had just happened. Sabrina had put the gun between Trevor's eyes. Rayne watched his expression. He was smiling, thinking it was a joke. Sabrina wasn't joking and pulled the trigger.

Rayne saw the blood and felt the warm, crimson fluid wet her face. She was right next to him. Trevor's blood and bits of his cranium were all over Sabrina and Rayne.

Bernadette was in the room with them. She didn't say a thing. They cleaned up and got rid of Trevor's body. Their bond was stronger than the man who brought them together. It was till death, Trevor's death, Dora's death and beyond.

We were sharing Trevor, Rayne thought, just me and

Sabrina though. That had been the unspoken rule. Trevor fucked Dora Dean. Sabrina would've killed Dora if it weren't for the fact that Trevor damn near forced his dick into her. Either way Trevor got his brains blown out every way possible. Rayne laughed.

The cops in the precinct stared at her like she was crazy.

She screamed. "All of us are crazy."

The Fatal Four were no more. Dora Dean was dead. Rayne didn't know exactly how it happened. There were only three of them left.

The detective told her a bit but didn't reveal too much. Rayne knew Sabrina and Bernadette weren't saying shit. Her girls would keep their mouths shut and she wouldn't say shit either.

Rayne wished she knew more about the law. Sabrina was smart and Bernadette had been in jail so many times that she knew the judicial system backwards and forwards. The medication paralyzed her mind.

Rayne closed her eyes.

four

Bernadette had so many holes in her body. She had been shot four times.

"I've got a hole in my ass, one in my pussy, two in my nose and two in my ears. Lord knows I didn't need anymore," she hissed.

Bernadette wasn't sure whether Sabrina was alive. She didn't know where Rayne had been taken. She knew Dora Dean was dead. She had to be. Bernadette was sure the two bullets she heard while trying to get out of the kitchen ended her life. Dora face down on the floor was the last glimpse of her Bernadette had. There was no way she could've recovered from that onslaught.

Bernadette didn't wanna be where she was. She wanted to escape her perdicament. She wanted to run out but that was

virtually impossible.

A cop was stationed right outside the hospital room and her swollen right ankle was shackled to the bed. Bernadette wasn't in any condition to attempt an escape even if it was a possibility. She knew it wasn't. Her left leg was elevated. She'd gotten shot in the back of her thigh. Bernadette also took a bullet in the right arm and one in her right shoulder.

She had multiple surgeries and all of the bullets were removed. Her injuries weren't as bad as they appeared. She'd been in the hospital for three days and was already able to move her right arm and wiggle her left toes. The dyke was in a lot of pain and was heavily sedated. It didn't bother her much. Bernadette was always on something. She was a habitual weed smoker, already addicted to Tylenol pm and she was an alcoholic.

The last thing she remembered was Rayne driving to the hospital and hopping out to get help. Bernadette's injuries rendered her unconscious. When she woke up she found herself lying on a hospital bed handcuffed by the ankle, heavily medicated and looking into the face of a female officer.

"You have the right to remain silent. Anything you say can and will be used against you in a court of law. You have a right to an attorney…do you understand these rights?"

Bernadette closed her eyes, blocked the voice out of her mind and silently cursed her faith. She'd been arrested more times than she cared to remember. She knew the drill. However this time things were different.

Everything went wrong from the beginning. Once they walked inside that crack house, it was like they were expected. Dora Dean knew something was wrong. It was dark in the front room, no lights were on. She'd been inside the house but never seen it completely dark before.

Bernadette saw a bat hit Dora over the head. It wasn't a very good swing but it got her good enough. A dude was creeping up on Sabrina. She saw him before he could get to her.

Sabrina towered over the dude. He had a golf club. Sabrina aimed the shotty in her hand. He ran towards a leather sofa. Sabrina pulled the trigger. The shotgun's slug exploded into a side of the sofa. The dude made it to the other side just in time.

Sabrina still heard the guy breathing heavily and cursing. He didn't sound like he was in any pain.

"Shit! They knew we were coming." Bernadette yelled.

"Check on her," Sabrina yelled back.

Sabrina had already found the light switch on the closest wall to her. She turned the lights on then quickly surveyed her surroundings. She was tall and threatening carrying a twelve-gauge, double-barreled shotgun. The guy who attacked Dora with

the bat ran to the rear of the house.

Bernadette reached down and helped Dora up. Bernadette was strong. Dora wobbled but was conscious. She moaned a bit but never gave in.

"Let's go get that cash," she'd said cocking back the hammer on her 32 revolver. "Steve Stunner hit me with that bat. I'm gonna smoke his ass."

Those were the last words Bernadette heard out of Dora's mouth. They went into the kitchen. They should've run right out of the house and aborted the mission. They realized niggas knew what was going on. They should've had Rayne with them.

If Rayne had gone in with them things would've went differently. Rayne's crazy, Bernadette thought. She would've carved her way though them niggas with that machete and we would've all been alive. Bernadette cursed herself for not being able to save Dora. Steve Stunner had it out for her.

They underestimated him. The four of them had done too many robberies and gotten away with them. They were way too sure of themselves. Bernadette knew they didn't plan the Steve Stunner spot rush as well as they'd planned the others.

In hindsight, Dora Dean should never have been sent in to spy. Sabrina would've been the best person working the inside. She was way smarter and would've seen more than Dora ever could. Rayne should've rushed the spot with us and Dora should've been the getaway driver. Dora was a better driver anyhow. Bernadette thought.

    Things were what they were. It mattered little now.

    "Cop," she said with a hoarse voice.

    It was the first time she'd said anything. The officer didn't hear her. Her voice was weak. Bernadette gathered more strength. "Cop," she repeated.

    The officer turned and acknowledged. It was the same one Bernadette saw when she opened her eyes the other day. Bernadette was pretty sure they were rotating shifts. She didn't even know what time or what day it was.

    "What is it?" The officer asked.

    "Where are my friends?"

    "Worry about yourself."

    "You fucking dirty ho. You look more of a dyke than I do."

    Bernadette wasn't in much shape to do anything but stay right there fuming. When she was healthy enough to go, they were going to send her straight to court and directly to prison.

five

Sabrina had nothing to do but think. She was feeling awful. There was a bullet lodged somewhere in her midsection near her stomach and she was being nourished intravenously. She was still in the hospital. There was a cop right at the foot of her bed. As soon as Sabrina opened her eyes the officer read her, her rights.

After the cops read her rights he asked, "What happened to you girls in that house?"

"I have the right to remain silent." Sabrina worded weakly.

The officer gave Sabrina some hope. He'd asked what happened and it was like the Fatal Four were victims instead of the other way around. Sabrina's mind drifted back to thinking about

Dora Dean and the others. She wanted to know if Rayne and Bernadette were okay.

"Are my friends okay?" She asked the cop with genuine concern.

His chair was at the foot of the bed. Sabrina realized that one of her ankles was cuffed to the hospital bed.

"One of your friends is dead ...Got shot twice in the head, execution style. The other two are alive. One of them is here in this hospital with you and the other is in custody."

The officer was young, very attractive and black. Sabrina instinctively reached a shaky hand to the scar Rayne had given her, the scar that destroyed her beauty.

"How'd you get that nasty scar?" The officer asked.

"Huh...? What's your name?" Sabrina asked.

The officer pointed at the shield on his chest then said, "Officer Everett, Clarence Everett, and your name's Sabrina Murray."

"Yeah, I'm in deep shit right?" She asked.

Sabrina didn't trust the police, not even a little bit but there was something different about Clarence Everett. She wanted information. She wanted to know exactly what was ahead for her and her girls.

"I don't know. I think if you keep quiet things will just go dead. You girls were in a bad neighborhood and dealing with a bad man, Steve Stunner. That's what they call him. Why were you girls there?"

"He was holding us hostage," Sabrina lied. "He had me and the one who died, Dora Dean. Regardless of what the other girls say, the truth is I was the only one who did anything. I shot whoever and whatever was done I did it. Fuck the right to remain silent. I don't want them to go down for something I did. We were victims but I'm the one who did shit."

"What did you do?" the officer asked.

Sabrina wasn't even sure what the authorities knew. She mentally rewound the events.

There was an ambush as soon as they walked into the house. Dora Dean was hit in the back of the head with a bat. Her attacker ran towards the kitchen. Even in the dark Dora was still able to identify Steve Stunner. Sabrina remembered finding a light switch and turning it on. There was another man with a golf club. He swung it out of fear. He must've seen the shotgun. She fired off at him but missed. He sought cover behind a sofa.

Sabrina told Bernadette and Dora to go after Steve. They would go into the kitchen and get that box with all the cash in it. They should've left then. Sabrina was very bold and figured they could handle things. They needed that money.

More dudes were coming down a flight of stairs. One fired a pistol. Sabrina returned fire. She missed him but a bullet hit her in the gut. Sabrina was hardboiled and as stubborn as a mule. She stood there while the guy was moving closer and firing his

weapon. She let the empty shells fall from the shotgun and to the floor. She calmly reloaded the shotgun. Sabrina let off the shotty. His cap was peeled back and his head exploded.

Sabrina wasn't going anywhere until Bernadette and Dora came back. She heard shots fired in the kitchen. She saw Bernadette run back out. She was shot. Bernadette and Sabrina heard two shots. That was when Dora was shot in the head. Sabrina didn't know what had gone down in the kitchen. All she knew was that Steve Stunner had gotten them good. He had murdered Dora. Sabrina and Bernadette began backing themselves right out of that hell-house.

"You okay?" The officer asked.

"No!" Sabrina snapped. "I'm all fucked up. I don't wanna say anymore."

"You said enough," he said and moved away from the bed. He got on his walkie-talkie. Sabrina listened but wasn't sure what was going on. She closed her eyes and thought of Dora Dean.

Dora was the best looking of them all. Only the scar on Sabrina's face made her runner-up. Without the buck-fifty on her face, Sabrina was Beyonce. Sabrina was feeling horrible. Her body was on fire, her stomach was about to explode, she had a high fever. Dora must've messed up, she thought. Steve Stunner and his peoples were prepared for us.

Sabrina wondered about the relationship Dora had with Steve. Dora was sent on the inside this time. Pussy didn't easily sway Steve like it did other drug dealers. He was really cautious. Dora had to fuck him for the longest time. One day, Dora told Sabrina that Steve reminded her of Trevor. Sabrina had smacked Dora's face.

"Don't ever mention that nigga again!" Sabrina remembered yelling.

Dora was holding her wounded cheek while moisture built up around her eyes.

"Sorry Sabrina, I won't say his name again."

"See that you don't, bitch." Sabrina recalled saying that before storming off.

The only one who wasn't scared of Sabrina and her temper was Rayne. Even Bernadette was leery of Sabrina. They were all crazy. Rayne was just the one who was diagnosed and on meds. Rayne wasn't scared of shit.

Sabrina wasn't sure if it was a wise thing to speak to the officer. She figured it would put the blame on her instead of her girls. She wasn't even sure what they would be blamed for. Sabrina figured she'd cry self-defense when the case went to court. Sabrina knew she'd murdered the guy who shot her. His head was blown completely off of his body. She'd used her dick, the twelve-gauge double-barrel pump. The shit had never failed her.

They'd failed and for the first time the Fatal Four suffered a fatality. Dora Dean is dead Sabrina thought. "They got my girl Dora." She uttered.

six

When Trevor got Sabrina pregnant, she was kicked out of her house. The year was '95. One year after Sabrina was sliced. Trevor showed balls asking Rayne if Sabrina could live with them. Rayne was crazy enough to agree. She always did what Trevor requested. He didn't ask for much.

Trevor wanted Rayne to hold him down. He lived with Rayne and her crack-head aunt in the Bronx until her aunt got murdered by her husband. Afterwards it was just Rayne and Trevor. He sold drugs in Brooklyn but he wasn't very good at it as far as Rayne could tell. She was making more money shaking her ass and swinging on poles at strip clubs then he did hustling.

In the beginning, Rayne was a skinny thing with nice hips.

She had a small booty and cute face. Her long hair was a plus when she worked the pole. Rayne would whip her long hair around until the sweet scent of the shampoo she used enveloped the strip-joint. She made good money.

Trevor urged Rayne to prostitute herself. She knew he had a few bitches out on a strip in Brooklyn. She'd do anything for him but she'd never sell her ass. Rayne had suffered through her own biological father's abuse and wasn't about to allow just any man to take her body. A customer had followed her out of a strip club one night. He had given her so much tip-money and had a lap dance in the VIP room.

Rayne got atop him where he sat and grinded her bubbly ass until his dick was so erect she had to move her butt to the side to avoid getting poked. He whipped his dick out but she wasn't into that.

"Fuck that bitch!"

He pulled two fifty dollar bills out of his pocket.

"Jerk me off and I'll give you a hundred dollars."

Rayne was tempted but she shook her head. Later, he followed her while she was walking to the train station and forced her into a deserted alley.

He tried to push her down to the ground. All the pole work gave Rayne strong calves and thigh muscles. She resisted. The guy smacked her down. Out came the knife Rayne carried. She always had some sort of blade handy. Poor guy was ill fated.

He saw the knife in Rayne's hand and laughed in her face. A straight kick sent her flying backwards. He jumped on her and flipped her over. The man kept her head to the concrete with a hand and kept her ass straight up in the air with an arm.

Rayne was wearing a skirt that night. He'd managed to tear her panties off in the struggle but should have paid more attention to the knife. Rayne figured he thought she'd dropped it already. Rayne never dropped a knife in her life.

He had a finger in her pussy. Rayne didn't take her medication that day. The assault had her seeing blood. He was busy trying to force himself in with his hard dick. Rayne allowed him to think that she wasn't gonna resist. Then she squirmed and struck out with her knife.

The blade slid up and then down the underside of his penis. Blood splattered, it seemed to move in slow motion. She moved so fast the blood didn't get a chance to sprinkle the sidewalk. Before the dude could scream out, Rayne grabbed his bloody dick and brought the knife down with all her strength.

His dick was cut in the middle; it was still hard. He let out a guttural scream like a wild animal. Rayne went at his face with her knife. He struggled to push her away while getting sliced up in the worse way. It was all he could do to keep her off him. He swung blindly. His fist connected knocking her backwards.

Blood flew from her mouth. Her head snapped back hitting the side of a dumpster. Rayne was dazed but heard his moaning

and panting. She shook her head, groggily trying to get up but couldn't.

The guy was on his knees attempting to stand up. Both him and Rayne rose at the same time.

Rayne's panties were on the ground and her skirt was disheveled around her waist. His blood was on her hand, skirt, shirt and jacket. He was holding what was left of his penis and backing away. She realized she'd cut most of his dick off when she let go of the piece she had in her hand. It fell to the ground.

He looked at the piece of his dick on the ground. Rayne saw the fear in his eyes. Rayne gave him a growl. He knew he was fucking with an animal. He turned and started running. Rayne ran after him and stabbed him in the back before he was completely out of the alley. He kept running, the knife still in his back. Rayne broke out in hysterical laughter.

"Come back with my knife nigga!" Rayne yelled. "You want some pussy now huh?" She cried then started to laugh. "You still want pussy...?"

Rayne took the train home. She was all bloody and crying and laughing like a crazy bitch. People were looking at her. She shunned cops even then, even before she became apart of the Fatal Four.

She walked inside the crib the next morning. Trevor was out hustling or pimping as usual. Sabrina was home. They hadn't spoken to each other. Trevor would go to the living room and fuck

Sabrina. Then he'd be back inside the bedroom sleeping with Rayne. Sabrina was four months pregnant. It was the weirdest and craziest shit.

Sabrina saw Rayne. She looked bloody and horrid like Carrie on prom night. Sabrina spoke to Rayne for the first time.

"What the fuck happened to you?" She said with more curiosity than concern.

"I cut his dick off," Rayne said.

Rayne went insane. She began screaming like a white bitch in a horror flick. Sabrina hugged her and guided Rayne to the bathroom. There she ran a bath for her. Rayne stripped off her bloody clothes and got into the water. Sabrina washed the blood and filth of the night off in silence.

The next morning they spoke again. Trevor was shut out on the pussy-game from both of them for three months. Sabrina and Rayne had bonded. Their relationship became something so strong, not even Trevor could sever. A month after Rayne's horrible experience, Sabrina suffered a miscarriage. Rayne was with her during the ordeal, much the same way Sabrina was with her the night she came home bloody. Surrounded by two dangerously demented women, Trevor kept his distance. He got less cautious when they allowed him to fuck them again. Soon all three of them were in the bedroom, on the bed but Sabrina and Rayne never touched each other.

Sometimes Rayne would hold Trevor's dick while Sabrina

sucked the tip of it. When they were feeling really freaky they would do him at the same time. Sabrina would be sitting on his face, letting him use his tongue on her clitoris or up in between her vaginal lips and Rayne would ride him cowgirl style. Sabrina didn't allow Trevor to bust off inside her again.

"If you ever come in me, I'll kill you," She had told him one day.

One night Trevor yelled, "I'm coming," while digging out Sabrina. He didn't want to pull out. She pushed him off just in time to see his sperm squirting everywhere.

Rayne had to duck in order to prevent getting it in her hair. Sabrina didn't want any kids from Trevor. She wasn't enjoying her life and felt ugly. The scar on her face caused Sabrina to lose any sort of hold she had on herself. Her father had died. She'd lost her mother's friendship. Now she only had Trevor and Rayne.

Rayne allowed Trevor's sperm swimming up in her all the time. Rayne had never gotten pregnant for some strange reason. She once visited a gynecologist and was told that something was wrong with the eggs in her uterus. Further confirmation tests were necessary. Rayne switched gynecologists, never bothering to find what her problem was.

seven

Sabrina had taken the fall for her girls. She didn't get a heavy sentence because the system didn't have enough evidence to work with. They never found Steve Stunner and everyone inside the house was dead. Sabrina told the court that Steve Stunner had held her and Dora Dean captive for a week and Rayne and Bernadette had traveled from New York for the purpose of rescuing them. She threw herself at the mercy of the court. She promised to cooperate with the investigation.

Bernadette's and Rayne's situations went entirely different. The judge wanted to know why they didn't go to the authorities. Sabrina told the judge that if they'd have done that, Steve Stunner would've killed them. Bernadette and Rayne said nothing. Their appointed lawyers did the talking. Once Sabrina agreed to take

the rap, it became a cake walk for the other girls.

Most of the charges were dropped. Luck was on the side of the rest of the Fatal Four. Dora Dean was gone but only Sabrina was supposed to spend any sort of time locked up. She did a six month prison bid. Rayne originally had to spend three months in a facility for people with mental problems. During her stay, she beat up a girl and one of the faculty members. She wound up staying an additional nine months and spent some time confined to a windowless room alone, then in general population. She served more time than Sabrina and Bernadette combined.

Rayne found herself on a Grey Hound bus heading back to New York City from the mental facility. She didn't know where her friends were. Sabrina and Bernadette had never written her or visited. Rayne hadn't seen them since their frantic drive to the hospital. All she knew was that Sabrina had taken the fall for them and that Dora Dean was dead.

It was the year 2000 in the middle of November. There was snow on the ground. The bus wound its way slowly through the mountains. Finally, they reached the outskirts of New Jersey. Rayne was very anxious to get home even though she didn't really know where home was. She'd contacted her mother who was drunk as usual. She invited Rayne to come home. Rayne had nowhere else to go. Steve Stunner was on her mind as well. She still wanted to avenge Dora's death. She didn't know what her life was worth anymore. She hadn't much of anything before and now she felt like she had less.

Rayne's body had thickened in all the right places. Men looked at her more than ever. She felt prettier than before. Rayne was horny. She hadn't been with a man in more than a year.

When the bus pulled into the port authority Rayne had the biggest grin. She missed New York. She walked around the streets of Manhattan. Snow was on the ground and just as soon as she hailed a cab it began to lightly snow. She loved the winter and enjoyed the snow.

"Twenty-three forty-five University Avenue in the Bronx," Rayne said to the cab driver.

She looked outside the window, at the city she hadn't seen in some time. Nothing seemed to have changed. Besides the obvious physical transformation, Rayne wasn't sure what other changes she made but she felt different.

On her way to the Bronx she thought about getting her GED and furthering her education in college. She'd read a lot of books during her stay in the mental facility. Rayne realized Trevor had taken more things from her life than he'd provided. There was a whole world out there. She read about it and wanted to experience it. Rayne was scared since she had no experience. She felt all she could do was swing a blade, rob and strip, in any order.

When Rayne reached her destination, she paid the cab driver and hopped out the cab. She should've just rented a hotel

room but Rayne didn't have much money. Sabrina, Bernadette and Dora Dean had been her family. They used to feed themselves on robbing drug dealers.

"Rayne," she heard her name.

She turned around, didn't recognize the man at first. He was halfway down the block when he yelled her name. He came running towards her. She knew who he was.

"Angel…"

She remembered him. Angel was a very cool guy, handsome, always kept a job and stayed out of trouble. "I haven't seen you in a long time."

"How have you been?" He asked.

Angel graduated from high school and went to college in Albany to study auto mechanics. He returned home in the Bronx and started working at a garage. He had always been cute.

"Good and bad," she said. "You look good."

"So do you," he said giving her the once over. "You gained some weight and in the right places," Angel smiled. "I heard that you killed three people out in Philly and they had you locked up in a mental institution."

"It wasn't like that but that's how people talk." Rayne laughed and changed the subject quick. "I'm thinking about going back to school. You know how I've been running around and not doing anything but getting into trouble."

Angel ran a few of his fingers through his curly hair. Rayne was very attracted to Angel. His actions caused sexual fantasies to course through her horny mind.

"You were always getting into something Rayne. I heard you were robbing banks or something like that. This dude up on Fordham said you set one of his peoples up. He said you and some girls took his money and his drugs, ran up on him with masks on and guns."

"You can't believe everything you hear?" Rayne's street instinct immediately kicked in. "Who did you hear all that shit from, anyway?"

Angel eyed her curiously and answered. "I'd rather not say. I heard 'bout that shit a year ago."

"I ain't the girl I was a year ago." Rayne wasn't sure if she was telling Angel the truth. She didn't know who she was anymore. "What have you been up to?"

"Work… I ah just bought a house and ah… thinking of getting married."

"Really," Rayne sounding disappointed. "I remember playing run, catch and kiss with you when we were younger. Have you learned how to kiss yet?"

Angel laughed. "I think so… I've been told… Ah where are you headed, upstairs to your mom's?" He asked looking up at the building.

"Yeah, but I ain't gonna stay long. I don't wanna stay here. I don't like being around the neighborhood. I'm looking to change

up and do something different." Rayne thought about something then asked, "Have you seen Bernadette around?"

"Bernie," Angel said reflecting. "I forgot how close you two ah... were."

"Not that close," Rayne said with cynicism.

Angel knew what Rayne was talking about and laughed.

"I know you don't get down like that." Angel said smiling.

He was pleased with the way Rayne looked. She could tell by the way he licked his lips. "You really look good, Rayne. You've been taking care of yourself."

"Finally right," she said displaying herself to him with a spin. "I ain't stripping no more and I ain't messing with no dumb niggas. I wanna just get a fresh start. I don't wanna be around a place where rumors are being spread about me, you know?"

"I understand," Angel said. He thought about something. "Bernie works at this bar in Manhattan. She's a bouncer there."

Rayne laughed. "Are you serious Angel?" Rayne kept laughing nearly crying in the process. Angel gave her the location and the name of the bar. She said. "I know you said something about marriage but I don't really have many friends. I've deaden whatever I had a year ago."

Rayne thought about what she had said and wondered if it was a lie. Her pussy was quivering. Being close to a hot-looking man aroused her. She wasn't sure what he thought of her. Rayne was confident she was looking good. She could tell Angel was feeling her from the way he was eyeing her.

"I wanna go see Bernadette but I don't wanna go anywhere alone," she offered.

"It's still early, Rayne," he said. "I gotta go to work in a couple of hours."

"I'm not talking about right now," Rayne laughed. "How about later on today, does she work at night?"

"She does."

"Would you mind accompanying me to the bar?" Rayne asked as sweetly as she could. Before Angel could answer she asked. "Are you engaged or something?"

"No, but I got a girlfriend," he said shyly.

"Maybe you need a woman and not a girl who is a friend," Rayne said with sass.

"She's a woman," he laughed.

"So am I," she said boldly.

"I see that you are." Angel's cell phone rang. He reached inside a pocket and looked but didn't answer it. "Here." He pulled out his wallet and gave Rayne a business card. "My cell number, call me tonight. My garage isn't too far from here."

"Your garage…?" Rayne asked sounding impressed.

"I'm trying, Rayne. Look I gotta go. I guess you'll call me later?"

"I sure will, Angel. It was good seeing you. And it'll be better seeing you later," Rayne said.

They both smiled. Angel walked away.

She watched him hop inside a beautiful BMW. Rayne stood in the front of her building watching. A sigh escape her when Angel was gone.

Rayne realized that she'd been nervous talking to Angel. He had gotten closer to the real Rayne than any other man had gotten in a long time. Most men just got the fabricated Rayne, the actress, the spot rusher. The Fatal Four would seduce drug dealers, becoming their play things. Angel's car reminded her of a drug dealer's.

Once Dora Dean and Rayne had tag-teamed a huge dealer, Hooey Jameson, down in St. Louis. They used to sleep with him at the same time. He loved women and once urged them to eat each other. Rayne didn't wanna do it but Dora pulled her aside and said, "Listen we gotta do this. We here to earn his trust..." It sounded right to Rayne but she knew Dora was attracted to her and just wanted to get between her legs. Dora was such a sexual being.

They murdered that dude in St. Louis. He didn't give up his money and jewelry without a fight. If it weren't for how manly and strong Bernadette was Rayne wasn't sure of how things would have turned out. Their situation with Hooey Jameson was a close call. Steve Stunner was a tragedy.

"Rayne..."

She heard her name being called. Rayne looked and

grimaced. She definitely didn't want to speak with the person. Rayne quickly ran right inside the building.

eight

Rayne knocked on the door. Her father answered. Rayne instantly got scared and angry. The two emotions she always felt whenever she was around him.

"Hey," he greeted with delight. "It's my little girl." He reached out to hug her.

"Fuck off," Rayne said pushing through the door past him.

Rayne didn't even look at him. She dared not. She was afraid of what she'd do if he touched her again. She might let him strip her, bend her over and fuck her like he used to do. Maybe she'd beat him to death. She had killed a man before. Her father was a weak man, had always been. The heroin had left him in terrible shape and the methadone had depleted him of all his strength. Even so, he was still the monster she'd grown to fear

and loath.

Walking into the apartment had Rayne thinking back to when she was 13 years old. She was home from school and her mother wasn't there. Her mother worked two jobs and was hardly home. Her father never worked. He'd suffered an injury in the military and used that as his excuse for not working again. He didn't even take out the garbage.

When Rayne got home from school she would sometimes go to her room and he'd be there waiting for her. He would order Rayne to get naked or slowly stripped her. He would then force her to lie on her stomach. He'd put a pillow over her head and fucked her from behind until he was good. Sometimes it didn't last longer than a minute, but there were times when the assault would go on for a half hour.

Afterwards Rayne would run to the bathroom and take a bath. She endured that treatment since twelve years old until she left at fifteen. Rayne told her mother but her mother chose not to believe Rayne or her sister, Riley.

Her father was a very handsome and charismatic man with a twinkle in his eyes before he left for Desert Storm. After the war, she wondered why her mother tolerated him. Rayne had no idea of how old he was but knew her mother came from Puerto Rico when she was thirteen. By the time her mother was fifteen years old her father had already impregnated her. Rayne hated both her parents. The smell of alcohol was on her mother's breath when she greeted her. Rayne pushed out of the hug.

"It's the same shit." Rayne said to her. "No wonder I'm so fucked up."

Rayne went straight to what was once her and her sister's room. When she opened the door she was shocked to find Riley sitting on the bed they used to share.

"My fucking God," Rayne exclaimed with surprise and delight. "Riley!"

She hadn't seen her sister in over three years. Riley had gotten married when she was eighteen and moved to Florida. Her husband was a good looking military man. He wasn't like their father.

"Pee-Wee," Riley shouted. She hopped off the bed and gave Rayne a big hug.

The sisters held each other while crying then laughed. Riley took a good look at her younger sister.

"You look good Pee-Wee. You gained mad weight. When I saw you last you looked anorexic."

"I know Riley," Rayne began crying again. "I've been through so much shit. I hated you for leaving me here to deal with all this shit. But you were smart to leave."

"I didn't want to but I had no choice." Riley began crying again. "I don't wanna talk about what used to be. Mother told me you were coming home today and I took the first flight I could to New York. I arrived yesterday. I want you to come to Florida and

live with me."

Rayne stared at her sister. She didn't know what she wanted to do. All she'd known was what Trevor told her and what Sabrina suggested. Bernadette also gave her advice. Only Dora Dean, who was just as screwed up as Rayne, didn't. Dora had been raped more times than Rayne and Riley combined.

Dora once told Rayne she was fucked by ten men, one after the other. Rayne had cried while Dora was telling the story. Dora described it in great, bitter detail, down to how her ass leaked blood for weeks after.

Dora used to fuck around with a drug dealer. She was living with him and one day rivals broke down the door to his project apartment looking for him. They didn't find him. They kidnapped Dora, blindfolded her, raped and assaulted her for weeks. They did it repeatedly until Dora was almost dead. She was only sixteen.

That was the reason Dora didn't care about her body, Rayne thought. Dora used to do most of the dirty work for the Fatal Four. She was the one who would seduce the men, let them fuck her while winning their trust. Rayne began crying again. Thoughts of Dora made her emotional. Dora had endured so much, thought Rayne. I'm gonna avenge your death.

"I can't go to Florida," Rayne said.

Rayne saw a diamond ring on her wedding finger and the wedding band. She wished she had met a man like Riley's husband. Before Riley could say anything else their father walked into the room.

Rayne jumped on her father. He couldn't even defend himself. Riley screamed.

"No," she pleaded as Rayne began beating him with her fists. "Don't do it, he's not worth it."

Rayne knew he wasn't but that didn't stop her from beating him. Rayne lifted his body up by the little hair on top of his head and shoved his head into a bedroom window. His head didn't go through, the glass didn't break. Rayne opened the window up.

"Let's see if you can fly motherfucker," Rayne yelled. "Didn't you used to tell people you were an Air Force pilot you fucking liar."

Riley and their mother held Rayne, trying to stop her from throwing her father out of the window. Rayne looked over at her mother like she was gonna beat her ass as well.

"Please!" Riley screamed and dropped to her knees crying her lungs out. That was the only thing that caused Rayne to simmer down.

"I can't stay here." Rayne said to no one. "I hate all of you."

Rayne angrily walked out the door.

Downstairs, she broke out in hysterical laughter. She walked over to a corner store and got herself a Sunkist soda and fumbled in the duffle bag she had and got her lithium and Zoloft.

She took her pills. She waited downstairs for the cops to arrive. They never did. Riley eventually walked out the building.

"I'm sorry." Rayne said to her.

"Sorry for what, for not killing him?"

Before Rayne could answer, Riley grabbed her younger sister by the arm. Rayne pushed away from her.

"Rayne, what the fuck are you gonna do, beat me up too?"

"No Riley," Rayne said with moisture forming in her eyes. "I'm not gonna harm you, ever. What does it look like upstairs?"

"It looks like you did what we should've done years ago." Riley hugged her sister. "You're coming with me."

"Where are we going?" Rayne asked.

"To my hotel room," Riley said taking a deep breath. "I rented a car." She pointed towards it. "We should go shopping."

"I don't have no money," Rayne told her.

"As long as I'm living Pee-Wee, you got whatever I have."

nine

Riley was staying in a hotel near Times Square. The sisters went to 34th street in Manhattan and shopped at Macys. Rayne had never shopped before with her sister and they had a lot of fun together. The last time Rayne purchased this much clothes was after the Fatal Four cleaned out Hooey Jameson in St. Louis. Hooey was a huge score but he wasn't their initial mark.

It all went down back in 96. Sabrina, Rayne, Dora Dean and Bernadette were at the Tunnel nightclub. Sabrina's favorite rap group, the Lox was performing. She loved the music and was enjoying the show. They were at the club scheming on Jadakiss, one of the group members.

Jadakiss lyrics were about selling and how well he flossed. Rayne had this idea to start rushing rappers. She figured the Lox

would be a good group to start with. They had discussed it with Trevor but he was reluctant to let the Fatal Four loose on the Lox. Sabrina argued against it because she had a crush on Jadakiss. The girls continued to debate the issue at the bar.

"You do the inside work, Sabrina. That way you can fuck Kiss," Rayne said.

Sabrina nodded with a smile when she heard that. Then touched her face and felt the scar. "He ain't gonna want me," she said.

"Look at your body, those legs and how tall you are girl. That nigga is gonna wanna get all up between them," Rayne encouraged Sabrina.

Bernadette nodded in agreement.

"Fuck you bitch. You're just saying that because you made me ugly," Sabrina yelled.

Rayne knew how sensitive Sabrina was. She loved Sabrina and a pang of guilt ripped through her. Sabrina was right. Rayne stared at the drink in her hand and remembered that she had not taken her meds. Her skin bristled beneath the tight dress she was wearing. Rayne was prepared to spit a razor if Sabrina got overzealous.

"Calm down ladies," Trevor rushed to settle them down. He knew that Sabrina and Rayne were both capable of killing each other.

"I'll do it," Dora Dean said ending the discussion.

Dora Dean looked deliciously good, they all knew Jadakiss would take one look at her and instantly want some. Trevor licked his lips at Dora. Dora gave him her best smile, showing perfect teeth. Sabrina leered at the both of them.

"That settles that," Bernadette said.

Trevor took his eyes off of Dora's flawless face and turned his attention to some dudes talking loudly, a couple of bar stools away. He could tell by their accents and the way they were dressed that they were from out of town. It was clear from their bling that they were holding dough. Trevor spotted a Rolex watch on one of them and the other pulled out a knot full of hundred dollar bills. Others eyed them but no one did a thing. Whoever the two out of town niggas were, they were serious, they were dealers, Trevor could tell.

One of them cracked a joke and the other one grinned. Trevor saw a mouth full of diamonds encrusted in his gold fronts. Trevor turned to Dora Dean.

"Forget about that Lox nigga. I think we found a better mark."

Dora patted her backside and pursed her lips, preparing herself. Before she could make her move, Trevor grabbed her.

"Wait," Trevor said.

Three hoochies with sex appeal rolled up on the dude with the diamonds in his mouth. He began tossing hundred dollar bills at them like Rick James at a strip joint. A satirical smile

creased Trevor's lips; they had found their next victim. He sized up the dude who obviously loved pussy. All the females were flocking around him, thinking that they'd be leaving with him and his partner. Trevor didn't want to lose this mark. He looked at the Fatal Four.

Even with the scar on her face, Sabrina was far more attractive than she gave herself credit for. Sabrina had the body of an Amazon. This time her body wouldn't be enough. Trevor's eyes settled on Rayne. Rayne was a nice looking thing. Trevor knew that Rayne could fuck like a rabbit.

"You Rayne," Trevor said glancing back. "You and Dora Dean," Trevor turned back to them and continued with the biggest smile. "No man will be able to resist the both of you."

Dora Dean and Rayne rushed Hooey Jameson. One month later Sabrina blew the brains out of his head, killing him. Hooey Jameson didn't go down without a fight. It took all four of them to take down his fat country ass.

Dora Dean and Rayne realized that Hooey Jameson was a strange nigga the moment they arrived in St. Louis. He lived in a huge mansion and most of the land was like jungle. There was a pool that had not seen water. Dora and Rayne thought that Trevor had misjudged Hooey. He might have had a mouth full of platinum and diamonds and wore a Rolex but that might have been about it. Just as soon as they walked into his run down mansion and put their bags down Hooey took them around the side of the house to his ten car garage. He showed them his collection.

"Bingo," Rayne whispered to Dora when the garage door electronically flipped open.

"Cha-ching-alinga-ling…" Dora replied.

He had two luxurious looking Mercedes, two posh BMW, and two pimped-out classic Cadillac's. He had a '67 Mustang and a '71 Corvette. Then there was a sweet yellow Lamborghini and a juicy red Ferrari.

One day, Rayne went out back and saw a huge dog house. She cautiously walked over to it, took a peek inside and saw a dog's remain. She ran back to the house and told Hooey.

"I knew I forgot something. I forgot to feed the fucking dog." The fat man said.

"You must've not fed him since you got him," Rayne said walking off and shaking her head.

She'd almost made it out of the room when she heard.

"Wait, you forgot something."

"What?" she asked.

"Come here bitch, you forgot to suck my dick."

Rayne shook her head. The fat bastard always wanted his dick sucked and she was growing tired of doing it. If it wasn't for her girls she would've never gotten on her knees that day.

Dora hated the Hooey Jameson job for other reasons. There were no air conditioners or screens for the windows at Hooey's mansion and it seemed all the insects in the city decided to migrate there. He had ceiling fans and all the windows remained opened. Hardly anyone came to visit.

Dora Dean and Rayne spent a whole week with him. Fucking and sucking him off, doing lesbian routines for him and his friends. His friends always tried to persuade Dora and Rayne to leave with them. They used jewelry, money and sometimes even the air conditioners inside their cars to bribe the girls. Rayne was tempted. She laughed once when she overheard Dora telling a friend of Hooey, "I'll suck your dick if you get Hooey an air conditioner."

They hated things in St. Louis. The day before they robbed and killed Hooey, Rayne called Sabrina up and told her that she wanted to quit. It was the very morning Sabrina and Bernadette arrived in St. Louis. Sabrina was pissed.

"Bitch we didn't take a flight all the way down here just so we can go back to New York empty-handed." Sabrina chastised Rayne. "Didn't you say we can catch the nigga alone tonight?"

"Yeah but," Rayne began.

"So we gonna get his ass tonight. What the fuck's wrong with you? You said his dick was small anyway."

Both Bernadette and Sabrina laughed.

"His dick is real little but he weighs over three hundred pounds. Every time he gets atop me he flattens me, I can't breathe. Not to mention how he sweats like a fucking animal. Bitch just let me come to the hotel room. I need some cool air, nigga ain't got no air conditioner."

Sabrina laughed and hung up the phone on Rayne.

"It's on and popping tonight," she smiled at Bernadette. "We gonna spot rush his fat ass."

ten

Rayne and Dora were excited to know the St. Louis job would be coming to an end soon. Sabrina and Bernadette had Hooey's address. Now all they had to do was find the damn place. Dora Dean had confidence in Sabrina.

"Don't you worry 'bout a thing, your girls will come through for you," Dora Dean said.

They spent the day working on Hooey's energy and were running out of condoms. Even though they loathed the fat dude it was work. Getting Hooey seemed like a cakewalk because he usually fell right to sleep after he rolled on top of one of them and did his business.

Hooey kept most of his prized possessions and money locked in a safe. The safe was in his main bedroom behind a picture frame that electronically moved to the side when you knocked a certain spot on the wall. Dora Dean and Rayne were the sneakiest of the four criminally inclined vixens, but didn't have the combination.

Rayne stayed downstairs and Dora was in the room with the fat man. Rayne heard rapping on one of the downstairs windows. She crept over.

"Who is that?" She asked.

"It's us bitch," Bernadette whispered.

Sabrina and Bernadette climbed in through the window.

"Where's he?" Sabrina asked.

"Upstairs with Dora... in the same room where the safe is... We don't have the combination," Rayne rushed with words.

"What were you guys doing all this...?" Sabrina began.

"Slow down, bitch. The nigga is strange and besides, ain't nobody gonna just give you the combination to their damn safe." Rayne snapped at Sabrina.

Rayne definitely had a point and Sabrina didn't push the issue any further. They weren't able to bring guns with them on the flight. They didn't have a gun connection in St. Louis. The minute Bernadette mentioned weapons Rayne went right inside her pocket and pulled out an old 32 shortnose revolver.

"I just happened to have found this in his basement," she smiled.

"Give me that," Bernadette said snatching the gun.

"I better take that gun," Sabrina said with her hand held out.

Bernadette didn't want to give Sabrina the gun. Sabrina had a shorter fuse than Rayne. Sabrina would shoot the fat man before they acquired the combination.

"I'll hold onto the piece." Bernadette said shutting down any further discussion. "What else you got?" She asked Rayne.

Rayne showed them an axe so massive she could barely carry it. And she had brass knuckles. Sabrina examined them and declared them hers. She slipped the knuckles on her left hand. Rayne had a long blade she kept for herself. No one was about to challenge her for it. Bernadette saw that Rayne had found a bat and decided to take that as well.

"We got duct tape." Sabrina worded to Rayne.

"I hope one roll of tape is enough," Bernadette stated to her girls.

"Let's do the damn thing," Sabrina snapped.

By the time they got upstairs, Dora was already dressed and ready to rumble. Hooey's mass was sprawled all over the bed snoring like a water buffalo. The Fatal Four stood around the bed looking down at him. Bernadette to the right clutching the bat, Sabrina to the left with her left hand full of brass, Rayne at the head of the bed with a knife and Dora had the 32 revolver.

Hooey's loud snoring was all that could be heard. They just stared, no one moved to do anything. Hooey was a big man.

Bernadette shook her head.

Dora moved closer to his nakedness. A white sheet covered half his sweaty body. Dora pulled the sheet back and the other girls almost shriek when they saw how small his penis was. Sabrina couldn't hold back and broke out in a laugh. Hooey opened his eyes.

"What's so funny bitch?" He asked groggily.

"Your little dick, you fat ass motherfucker," Sabrina said.

"Surprise, this is you getting got." Bernadette always said this to victims.

Hooey was unexpectedly fast and raised his back off the bed. In no time he had a meaty hand wrapped around Dora's slender neck. Rayne reacted quickly by sticking her knife in Hooey's other hand. He was in the act of throwing a punch.

Rayne stabbed as hard as she could. The knife went through the middle of his palm. Hooey swung back and slapped Rayne in the face. Her body went flying across the room crashing against a wall. She was knocked out.

Hooey let go of Dora and yanked the knife out. He flung it after Rayne but the knife ended up stuck in the wall above her limp body.

Bernadette dropped the bat. She hammered her elbows and fists on Hooey as he tried to get out of bed. Sabrina hit him with her brass knuckled fist under his chin. The upper cut didn't slow him any. Dora backed up and aimed the gun. Bernadette

and Sabrina were too close to him for her to shoot. Dora wasn't the greatest shot.

Hooey took all that Bernadette and Sabrina had. He managed to get a good punch that sent Bernadette to the floor. Sabrina backed away warily.

"Is this the best you bitches got?" He boasted. "I'm gonna fuck every last one of you before I kill y'all." Hooey let out a guttural wail.

He never noticed Sabrina moving away from him so Dora could have a clean shot.

As he took a step towards Sabrina, Dora fired the 32. The bullet struck him in his back. He didn't even flinch even though there was blood. Hooey took another step towards Sabrina.

"Don't kill him," Sabrina screamed.

They needed the combination to the safe. Dora fired the revolver again hitting his left arm. Dora moved around, trying to get his attention. The third shot got his attention. Blood splattered on the floor where Bernadette was trying to shake off the punch. Hooey charged Dora. Dora lost her nerve and the gun fell from her hand.

"No!" Sabrina yelled.

She jumped on Hooey's back. He grabbed her by her hair before she could get a good grip and flipped her. Sabrina fell hard. Hooey stomped down hard with a wide barefoot, crushed her stomach. Sabrina felt a rib crack.

"Fuck!" Bernadette said reaching for the bat.

She charged him swinging the bat at his head and connected. Hooey grunted but didn't fall. The girls were amazed because he had been shot stabbed and thoroughly beat down. He was still standing.

Another swing hit the other side of his head, staggering him. He was stunned but managed to stay upright. Bernadette hit him in the knees. Hooey staggered yet refused to go down.

Bernadette hit him seven times before Dora pried the bat from her hands.

"Bitch, if you kill him we won't be able to get the combination to the safe," Dora yelled.

Hooey was finally on the ground. The onslaught from the bat was too much. He looked like a beached whale.

"You're right," Bernadette answered finally coming back to her senses.

Rayne didn't look bad. She was moaning while rising from the floor. Sabrina used a chair to get off the floor. Bernadette heard Dora scream and saw that Hooey was staggering back up.

"Damn!" Bernadette said in exasperation.

She hammered him with the bat. Hooey had gotten shot a few times. He was a beast. They didn't know what it would take to keep him down.

Dora scrounged on the floor for the gun. She would use every last bullet in it. The combination to the safe was not that

important now. Now staying alive was the only priority.

eleven

Rayne and Riley arms were filled with shopping bags. They lugged them to the hotel. Riley had a decent sized room. Riley and her husband were doing well for themselves. The sisters began checking out their purchases talking and catching up on old times. Riley knew her sister was a little bad ass but she never expected to hear the stories Rayne started telling. Rayne told her how Hooey Jameson was tortured for the combination to the safe.

"It was one of our bigger scores, Riley. Regardless of what we did, he wouldn't go down. Bullets, bats, brass knuckled, knives or damn fists and teeth and nails."

Back in Hooey's mansion, all the girls were standing. Some were wounded and tired. Sabrina clutched her injured ribs.

Bernadette held the bat in her hand.

Dora had the gun. Sabrina had warned her not to use it. She was determined to get the safe combination. Rayne was trying to pull the knife from out of the wall. It was stuck in the wall tighter than a nail. She tugged at it while the rest of the girls circled and stalked Hooey like hyenas.

"You bitches ain't shit!" Hooey huffed and puffed. "Y'all hating scalawags! What ya want?" He asked. He was bleeding from three bullets wounds. Hooey had been beaten up, there were knots on his face and his face was swollen. He didn't look like himself but he was still an obese and impressive mass. He stood with his fists balled up.

Sabrina grabbed the chair and ran towards him. Bernadette charged the fat man's legs. Dora followed suit. Rayne was still trying to get the knife out of the wall.

Bernadette hit Hooey below, clipping his legs. At the same time, Sabrina smacked him with the chair. Hooey was tall and massive. Sabrina missed his head and hit him on the side of a shoulder. She connected soundly. He stumbled. Bernadette and Dora wrestled him to the floor. Dora started raking Hooey's face with her nails and biting him.

Hooey was down on hands and knees. Dora was still scratching his already beaten up face with her nails and biting him on the head. Sabrina moved around his mass methodically, kicking him in his stomach. She was trying to get the air out of him. He grunted and coughed. She was succeeding.

He attempted to resume an upright posture. The girls were tiring and Hooey seemed to have gathered more strength. Rayne finally yanked the knife out of the wall.

"Yeah, motherfucker, yeah…!" She yelled in triumph.

Rayne joined the fight, but it was almost over. Bernadette jumped on Hooey's back like Sabrina had done earlier, but she was able to get her arms around his neck. The other girls backed off giving Bernadette room.

Hooey's naked mass was upright and leaking blood from everywhere. He was gurgling as Bernadette's strong arms tightened around his neck. He struggled for another three minutes before finally going down to one knee and then down to both knees.

"Give me the gun Dora." Sabrina requested breathing heavily. Dora didn't hesitate. Bernadette went for the chair Sabrina had hit Hooey with. Even though Sabrina had gotten him good, the chair was still intact.

"Sit down you nasty, fat, sweaty, little-dick-having, nigga." Rayne ordered. "Sit the fuck down!"

Sabrina held the gun to his head. Bleeding, he crawled over to the chair and sat.

Bernadette got behind him and held him in a choke hold while Dora and Rayne wrapped him to the chair with the duct tape.

"What's the combination to the safe?" Sabrina asked

waving the gun at him.

"Bitch I ain't telling you shit." Hooey laughed. "I'm gonna get you bitches, hunt you hos' down and kill every last one of you."

Bernadette punched him in his face. Hooey spat blood back at her.

"Use the bat bitch. Your punches are like kisses." He laughed. "Look at that little ass gun." He taunted. "I can take about ten more bullets and afterwards I'll shit bullets out, shit bullets on one of your faces. That's how we treat bitches down here in the Lou."

"I don't think he's gonna tell us shit." Rayne uttered.

"If he doesn't tell us, we're gonna have to kill his fat ass," Sabrina worded back. She was staring at Hooey with evil intent.

"Kill me bitch. I'm a die and you hos' ain't gonna get shit." He laughed. "Even my car keys are in the safe." He laughed even louder. "You bitches fucked up, y'all know y'all fucked up, y'all better kill me. Kill me, you ain't getting shit tonight. I'll die before I give a bitch shit. My dog was a bitch. I ain't even feed her." Hooey continued to laugh.

"What now?" Rayne asked sounding defeated.

No one spoke for some time. They weren't sure what to do. Hooey Jameson was a big deal in St. Louis but he had to die. Trevor always warned them about leaving a dealer with major street connections breathing after doing him dirty. The Fatal Four knew killing Hooey wasn't going to be the easiest thing. He wasn't about to give up anything. It seemed like a lost cause.

Dora had a solution. She left the room. No one knew where she went but she brought back a syringe and a bottle of bleach. Hooey looked into her eyes and took a deep breath.

"I'm tired of this shit," Dora spat with malice. "Me and Rayne been fucking his nasty black ass for a whole damn week. The nigga smells, he sweats, and he's all heavy. He be pumping that little twig and all you get is weight. Sometimes he don't even be all the way in. He just be hitting your thigh and shit." Dora opened the bottle of bleach and stuck the syringe in. She filled the syringe. "You gonna die slow and all horrible." Dora looked into Hooey's face. "Have you ever had bleach in your veins?" She asked him. "You're gonna be here suffering for two or three weeks spitting up blood and shitting green slime out your ass."

Sabrina moved closer to Dora. She had already decided to take Hooey as a loss and leave it at that. Sabrina wasn't sure about killing him.

"Enough" Sabrina said to Dora. "It's over lets get out of here."

Dora stared at Sabrina. She pumped a bit of the bleach out of the syringe.

"You damn right it's over bitch," she said putting the Syringe close to Hooey's neck.

"No," Sabrina screamed scuffling with Dora.

"If you spent a week fucking his fat ass you would be sticking this in him. You bitches can go back to New York. I'm gonna sit here and watch this little dick nigga suffer and die," Dora said in her most serious tone.

"Fine," Sabrina said warily eyeing Dora while backing away.

Dora stuck the needle into the flesh of Hooey's neck.

"Twenty-three left, once around forty-one right, thirty-eight right, seventy-seven left, clockwise nineteen…"

Rayne rushed right to the wall and hit it where she saw Hooey did. The picture frame whizzed, sliding away revealing the safe. Rayne remembered the numbers and turned the combination knob till the safe opened.

Dora laughed. She pulled the syringe out of his neck.

"I was gonna inject you with water you dumb nigga." Dora looked at her girls and took a dramatic bow. "Torture ain't physical it's all mental for a dumb nigga like him." She looked over at Hooey. "Water mother fucker, you gave up all your goods after getting shot and beat with a bat because I was gonna shoot water in you."

All the girls laughed. Rayne's attention was on the wads of cash in the safe. She pulled out knots of rubber banded hundreds. There was over one hundred thousand dollars plus lots of jewelry. Rayne grabbed a Rolex watch. It looked like the same one he was wearing at the Tunnel. She would give it to Trevor.

"We ain't never rushed a nigga who had this much," Rayne said.

Hooey gathered all of his strength and screamed out with one last ditch effort. The duct tape wrapped around his naked mass burst off him like an explosion. He rose like a mountain. The surge of strength he showed even had Bernadette pissing on herself.

Hooey roared and went after the girl closest to him. His fat fingers grasped at Dora. He managed to wrap both hands around her throat and squeezed as hard as he could. Dora shrieked in pain. Sabrina fired.

The top of Hooey head popped open spitting out blood and brains. Gore went all over Dora. Hooey was still standing and determined to snap Dora's delicate neck.

"Get him off me!" Dora gasped.

Sabrina shot him in the head again. Hooey's body was a bloody mess but he didn't budge.

Riley stared at her sister and said. "That's the craziest thing I've heard."

"Shoot, it was like we were in a damn movie and somebody hit the pause button." Rayne worded back to Riley and then continued her tale.

Bernadette struggled to remove his hands from around Dora's neck. She fell to the floor gasping for air.

Bernadette then kicked his still standing bulk in the chest.

It crashed to the floor. Finally he was dead.

For five minutes they stood looking at the corpse before Dora yelled at Sabrina.

"You could have shot me by accident!" She said with venom.

"I didn't," Sabrina's replied with indifference.

They scored bigger than they had ever did spot rushing. The girls all took the time to wash the blood off. Their bodies were black and blue but their pockets were swollen. The girls triumphantly left St. Louis in much haste.

Months later, Dora told the girls that she was having nightmares about Hooey's meaty fingers wrapped around her neck, squeezing and choking her.

"Hooey ain't even get a chance to do all that You should be having dreams about him on top of you smothering you with all that smelly fat and sweat, and that little ass dick." Sabrina said laughing. Dora gave Sabrina narrow eyes.

In Riley's hotel room, Rayne freshened up and changed her attire. Rayne had great skin and wore little to no makeup. She was excited and called Angel. He wasn't doing anything and agreed to take her to see Bernadette.

"I'm gonna look really pretty for you," Rayne said before giving him the address to the hotel all the while smiling.

"You really like this guy huh?" Riley asked seeing exhilaration all over her sister's face.

"I haven't been touched in a year, Riley." They hugged then both laughed.

twelve

It was 6 o'clock and dark already when a dolled-up Rayne pranced out of the hotel room.

"Be careful," Riley said.

"I always am," Rayne answered and waved.

She had to get used to the feel of walking in the three-inch stiletto boots she purchased earlier. Rayne watched the bustle of midtown from out a window while waiting for the elevator. Throngs of people sprawled a busy 42nd Street. Nighttime mattered little here It was always day time in Times Square.

The club that Bernadette worked for wasn't too far from the hotel. Rayne figured the planets were aligned. She was a bit nervous about seeing Bernadette but even more nervous about

seeing Angel. She wanted some dick. He had matrimonial plans but she was attracted to him. Most of all he wasn't a bad dude. She wanted to see what it felt like to fuck a good man. Not because it was a job or out of necessity like with Trevor. She stared at her reflection in the hallway mirror.

Her black dress was something really cute and revealing. It was Riley's choice. She had always dolled up to entice marks they were setting up. A sense of relief overcame her. Rayne realized she felt good because she was looking good and this was what she wanted to do.

Rayne was five feet six inches, one hundred and forty pounds of toned, hips, thighs and bubble ass. She'd never been as healthy as she was now. When Rayne and Riley were bonding earlier, she revealed to her sister that she wanted a vaginal piercing and a couple of tattoos. Riley had asked why in shock. Rayne explained it coolly. "I want it because I've never had anything like that before. I wanna have Dora Dean's name tattooed on my arm. I want people to look at it and see that I loved her."

After the Fatal Four rushed Hooey Jameson they went shopping and purchased shit they'd only seen bitches wearing in the movies and music videos. But that was far removed; the Fatal Four had more hard times then good ones.

Most of the dealers they robbed hardly had anything. That meant they had to do their robberies frequently and with more haste. There was less time for planning jobs as with the St. Louis caper. There were times when the Fatal Four would make up the plan as the job progressed.

They frequented popular strip joints and nightclubs where drug dealers, high rollers and ballers hung. They'd identified a mark and things would happen spontaneously. After Sabrina murdered Trevor they lost all sense of direction. Sabrina was smart but she couldn't spot marks the way Trevor did. He knew a good one when he saw one.

Riley bought Rayne a cell phone. She called it a late birthday present. Rayne spent her twenty fifth birthday in solitary confinement at a mental institution. Now a handsome man had her cell phone number. He called her when he was downstairs in front of the hotel.

Rayne was riding the elevator to the downstairs lobby along with two white men. They kept stealing glances at her body. She flirtingly rolled a couple of fingers through her bouncy hair. Both smiled. She sashayed from the hotel feeling better then she'd ever felt in her life. She saw Angel's BMW and rolled her hips as she walked.

"Hold on Rayne," he said lowering the window.

He hopped out the car, walked over to the passenger side and opened the door. Rayne felt good. She sat in the leather seat with a smile. She caught him looking at her ass before she sat, that made her laugh. Angel had got back in the driver's seat.

"What's so funny?" He asked buckling up his seatbelt.

Rayne said, "Come closer, I don't want anyone else to hear."

Angel moved his face closer and said, "No one is in here but us."

Rayne went in with her lips and kissed Angel. He resisted but only for a moment. She moved both her hands behind his neck, while her fingers trailed through his curly hair. She forced her tongue in his mouth. He hadn't opened his mouth as wide as she would've liked. He was resisting. Rayne wasn't sure why. Tonight she was downright irresistible.

When the kiss began to subside, Rayne dared to open her eyes. Angel's eyes were closed.

"Good," she uttered and took the time to kiss his nose.

"Bad," Angel said. "I gotta girl. I mean woman." Angel was blushing and it made Rayne liked him even more.

"I bet you she's an ugly thing, this woman you have," Rayne said jealously. "You got a picture of the bitch."

"I do," Angel said with a frown.

He whipped out his wallet and took out a photo and shoved it at Rayne.

"Oh," Rayne said examining the photo. "She's alright."

Angel's woman looked fully Puerto Rican and drop dead gorgeous and above that, they looked happy in the picture together. Rayne handed him back the picture. While he was putting his wallet away she reached down and put her hand on his crotch.

"You're still very happy to see me." Rayne bent as if she was speaking to his erect penis then she laughed. Angel was embarrassed and said nothing. Her wet and wild kiss had gotten considerable attention.

"Let's go see Bernadette," she said looking ahead. "I'm anxious to see the bitch."

The BMW pulled off. Rayne kept her attention off of him by playing with her new cell phone and looking around while he drove. Angel however, couldn't keep his eyes off of her. Rayne was never bold in relationships with men. She'd never really been in need of a man. Trevor didn't count. He was in a category all to himself. Rayne caught Angel glancing at her again while driving. She wanted a response and she'd gotten one. Rayne looked at him and smiled.

"You're still crazy, Rayne," he said smiling back.

Rayne crossed her arms and stared defiantly. She wasn't sure what she should do. She felt like punching him in the face. Yeah, she was crazy but she didn't like being called it. The thoughts blazed her mind. Her eyes were burning. She didn't like what Angel said. Her eyes saw nothing but red. Blood, she was beginning to see it.

"Are you okay, Rayne?" Angel asked sensing something was wrong. He looked at her and felt the tension increasing. "When I said you're still crazy, I meant it in a good..."

"What sort of good fucking way is calling a person crazy?"

She asked and continued before he had a chance to defend himself. "I know I'm fucking crazy. You don't have to remind me."

"Ah c'mon Rayne, you ain't crazy and if you are? So is everybody else in this fucking world. When we were young you used to do things out of the blue and you used to make things fun." He stared at her. "Remember we used to play in the sandbox together…?"

"The kids used to tease me because I didn't speak Spanish like them. I guess I was more Black than Puerto Rican." Rayne laughed. "Back then I hated you full bred Puerto Rican's. I was Black. I am Black and I'm proud of it. Back then I had to do things so that people wouldn't bother me."

"You kissed me and then grabbed my dick Rayne. Was that supposed to make me leave you alone?"

"I didn't grab your dick. I touched your pants." Rayne figured she was a bit too forward. She wanted Angel. She wanted him inside her. Rayne spent a good deal of her life taking what she wanted. Angel wasn't going to be as easy as rushing a spot.

BRANDON McCALLA

thirteen

He drove to 29th street, close to Madison Square Garden. Rayne had never been to the Garden in her life. She looked up at the lights and made a mental note to come down and watch the Knicks play. Angel quickly found parking. They exited the car and walked across 7th avenue to a sport's bar.

From the velvet rope outside, Rayne could easily tell this place was an upscale sports bar and not a dump. Rayne wasn't sure what to expect. All her girls became grimy due to their many horrible experiences. Rayne couldn't imagine Bernadette working in a place as well kept as the bar they were walking into.

Bernadette's past was shrouded in mystery. She never told anybody anything about herself. They all knew that she messed around with females. She'd often wished that she was a man. Bernadette was hard boiled.

Angel opened the entrance door for Rayne. She smiled thinking that Angel's actions were foreign to her. No other man had opened a door for her. Not even Trevor who never even gave her a 'bless you', when she sneezed.

"Thank you Angel," she said.

"Bernie is usually right here in the front," Angel said. "I hope she didn't take the night off. It doesn't matter. Let's sit at a booth," he said putting an arm around her waist.

Rayne allowed him to guide her body by her slender waist to a booth. After they were seated, a woman walked over and asked them what they were having. Rayne really wasn't paying attention to her. She was busy looking at the many television monitors showing hockey games. She noticed the occupants were mostly white. No one seemed to give Angel or Rayne a second glance. Rayne liked the place. It was nice. White people who didn't even know each other were laughing, drinking and talking like they were old friends.

"What do you usually drink?" Angel asked.

"Anything alcohol...What do you usually drink?"

"A Long Island iced tea or a beer to start things off."

"I'll have a Long Island iced tea, to start things off." She smiled at him.

The barmaid went to get the drinks. Rayne listened to the

rock music playing. She didn't know much about hockey, but she guessed it was a good game showing. The barmaid came back to them with their drinks and a menu of appetizers.

The drink was good but not too strong. Rayne used the straw and sucked it up like an alcoholic. She listened as Angel talked about his day and was enjoying herself. She wanted to smoke some weed but wasn't sure if Angel got down. Not wanting to seem ghetto she didn't mention it. She had not smoked weed in a year. The urge for a blunt was right up there with her urge for some dick. She thought about smoking weed while laying on her back with her legs up high and wide enough for Angel. She really wanted him to do something sexual to the situation between her legs.

Angel was halfway done with his drink. Rayne was playing with the ice in her empty glass with the straw. She motioned to the barmaid. She wanted another drink. As the barmaid was walking behind the bar, a man walked out of a door close to the bar. Rayne looked at the man really good. Something about him seemed familiar. First she thought she knew the dude. Then Rayne shouted. It wasn't a man. It was Bernadette. She glanced at Rayne.

Bernadette walked in the opposite direction, completely ignoring the woman waving her hands and yelling. She recognized Angel. "Cuz..." She uttered. She kept looking. The woman looked like Rayne.

"Oh my God...!" Bernadette sounded exasperated.

It was Rayne. Her hair was shorter and she looked different somehow but it was her. Rayne got out the booth and Bernadette could see her much better now. They stared at each other. All of a sudden, Bernadette ran and Rayne began running. They damn near knocked each other down when they collided. Rayne began crying and couldn't stop hugging her girl.

"I can't believe it's you," Bernadette said. She held Rayne at arms length in order to get a better look. "Bitch, you gained weight. You look fucking good." Bernadette looked over at Angel. "What the fuck is going on cousin?"

Angel said, "Surprise Bernie," and got out of the booth so that Bernadette could sit down with Rayne. They had a lot of catching up to do.

Angel walked away and Bernadette sat, Rayne said, "Why you didn't write me or come visit me you manly looking bitch?"

Rayne was still crying and a bit pissed. She was pissed and happy. They were tears of joy. Bernadette was right in front of her eyes. She reached a hand out and caressed the dyke's face, rubbing her and smiling. "I can't be mad at you bitch. But I was."

"I know Rayne. But you know the rules. When you go down there's no communication till you're out."

Bernadette recited one of Trevor's laws. Rayne shook off thoughts of Trevor as soon as they began.

"Sabrina," Rayne said. "Where is Sabrina?"

Bernadette took a deep breath. "Sabrina is still out in the streets like when we were the Fatal Four. She's with some dude out in Brooklyn where Trevor used to hustle. She's a gangstress now. She's been pimping girls on the strip. Ain't nothing changed for her. What about you, did you change?"

Rayne wasn't sure if she'd changed or not. Obviously Bernadette had. She looked well. The last time Rayne saw Bernadette she was on her death bed with four bullets in her. She still looked like a man. Her hair had grown longer but was corn rolled. She still had a mean face. Her breasts were undetectable and she still wore suits that a man would wear. Bernadette had the look of content in her eyes.

"So you work here?" Rayne asked.

"Yeah, I'm security but nothing goes bad around here," Bernadette said smiling. "You look great. You really do. I'm going to school." Bernadette added.

"For what...?" Rayne asked.

"Studying computers..." Bernadette laughed at herself. "I started getting into computers. This woman I mess with, she's the head of some Technology department at some company. She likes thugs but I ain't thugging no more. What went down in Philly changed me, Rayne. Dora Dean died and I lost all feelings for the shit. You know what I'm saying? I don't wanna get shot no more. I suffered bad and I walk with a limp now. You didn't see how I was walking?"

"No," Rayne said smiling. "You was running bitch. You still strong and look the same." Rayne thought for a minute then said. "I'm glad you ain't getting into no more trouble. I don't wanna get into shit anymore either. But I be thinking about Dora Dean. I still want closure."

Bernadette laughed. "Closure..." She said like it was a joke. "Rayne we got what we gave. We were robbing people and people fight back and kill when people try to take what's theirs."

Bernadette was being real. Rayne couldn't argue with her. Bernadette had definitely changed. Rayne wasn't sure if she'd changed or not. The conversation escalated and died down to idle chatter. Rayne still had the past on her mind, Trevor, Dora Dean and Sabrina. She really wanted to see Sabrina, wanted to be with Sabrina and Bernadette again like old times.

"I wanna go see Sabrina," Rayne said.

Angel had walked back over to the booth. Rayne ordered another drink. The barmaid walked over just as soon as Angel did and asked them if they wanted anything else. Bernadette told her not to bother bringing the check. The barmaid nodded. Rayne was gonna ask for another Long Island iced tea. Angel told Bernadette that it was getting late and time for him to head home.

"How's Gladys?" The dyke asked her cousin.

Oh that's her name. Rayne thought.

"She's fine." Angel answered.

Bernadette knew Angel was never a man who was short for words. She looked over at Rayne and saw that twinkle in her eyes. Bernadette laughed out loud.

"Let me find out that you two are fucking each other."

"Not yet," Rayne said with a sinister grin.

"No, I got Gladys remember," Angel said to his cousin.

He seemed uncomfortable. Angel grabbed his coat from the booth. Rayne figured it was her cue. She tossed on her coat. It was November. There was a fresh coat of snow on the ground. From the window, Rayne saw that it was softly sprinkling white outside.

"Bernadette, I wanna go see Sabrina," she said again.

"Tonight...?" Bernadette asked as if it was the worst idea.

Rayne figured now was a better time than any. She looked at Angel. She wasn't sure if he would drive them. Angel was easily swayed. He was way too nice. He called his woman up and told her that he was with his cousin Bernie. That seemed enough for the woman on the other side of the cell phone.

"Okay," he told Rayne and his cousin. "I'll drive you two to wherever but I ain't gonna stay for any length of time."

"That's cool," Rayne said with excitement. "I just wanna see my girl. I ain't seen her in a long time. I don't wanna be around where she's at for long. I don't wanna be like I was before, so I better not be around where I was."

It made sense. Bernadette gave Rayne a queer look. Some things haven't changed. She wanted to ask her if she was still taking her medication. She didn't dare ask that question in front of Angel.

At around ten that night, they left the sports bar hopped inside the BMW and drove out to Brooklyn. They were headed to the place where the Fatal Four was spawned. Rayne began reminiscing on Dora Dean.

fourteen

In the beginning it was Sabrina and Rayne. Trevor was pimping women and had some dope, crack and weed on the streets. He was a very successful drug dealer initially. Trevor was getting more money from prostitution than crack and dope combined. Soon the money started slowing down and wasn't enough for Sabrina, Rayne and Trevor to live off.

Trevor had a hot car, a great drug connect and two women who shared him and were willing to die for him. Rayne was always out in the hood with him helping him with his drug situation. Sabrina didn't care about that sort of thing. She was concerned about Trevor's affairs with the women he pimped. The unwritten rule was that Trevor, Sabrina and Rayne were together.

When Dora came to Trevor she didn't have anything. Her boyfriend had recently gotten killed. Dora's man had inadvertently gotten her involved in a caper that resulted in her getting kidnapped, beaten and repeatedly raped.

As soon as Rayne and Sabrina met Dora Dean and Bernadette they allowed them to make a square of their triangle.

Bernadette lived a block from where Trevor plied his trade. She was a dyke with a heavy reputation. She was selling drugs for Dora's man before he was murdered. When he died she linked up with Trevor. The Fatal Four was born.

Sabrina, Rayne, Bernadette and Dora Dean were the tightest unit. Trevor was the general behind this gangstress army. Every time Trevor had a problem with a local drug dealer or some pimp trying to muscle in on of his ho's, the girls were there to hold him down.

Bernadette was big and strong enough to fight a man one on one. Sabrina was always walking around with one of Trevor's guns. She was trigger happy. Rayne was the worst of them. Once Rayne got started it was hard to stop her. Rayne was always making things bloody. Dora rarely engaged in the physical stuff. Dora's job was to make sure Rayne didn't start spitting razors.

Between 1992 and 94, things were booming for Trevor. Then his drug campaign went completely downhill. He'd never been arrested. Trevor was too slick for the cops and detectives who were always roaming. However, he couldn't outsmart the

FBI.

Bernadette, Sabrina and Rayne were always getting arrested. Soon Trevor had no choice but to think about doing something else. Federal agents moved in on his prostitution strip and shut it down. Even with his army of hardboiled bitches, Trevor wasn't able to compete with a lot of other drug dealers in the area.

Sabrina and Bernadette initiated the idea to rush a rival dealer's spot. Trevor was against the plan because the dealer was connected. Trevor was running out of money, he had no bitches on the stroll and his drug connect abandoned him. Robbing drug dealers didn't seem like a bad prospect anymore. He had nothing but his girls who stood by him.

Dora volunteered her body. She let their first victim fuck her in order to gain his trust. Soon Dora was whipping the dealer's chromed-out Navigator.

Dora was irresistible. She was the reason Trevor had gotten a hole in his head. After falling for her seductiveness, Trevor wanted her sexually even as she tried to push him away. He treated the Fatal Four as if they were his property. That was a deadly mistake. He should have just left things like they were. Rayne's mind grappled with how it all went down. One thing was for sure, Sabrina and Rayne shared something that went beyond even Trevor. Sabrina unexpectedly put a bullet in Trevor's head.

Old memories flickered inside Rayne's brain like reels of

old short films. The past made her nervous. She looked outside and realized that Angel had stopped where they used to hustle. Immediately she spotted Sabrina. It was snowing and frigid outside. The cold was not a hindrance to people hustling out on the block.

The hookers' strip was two blocks away. Sabrina obviously was on her grind. Rayne saw what could only be crack heads doing a hand to hand exchange with a young chick. When the crack heads walked off she walked to where Sabrina stood like an Amazon in the hood.

A lot of people were crowded around her outside a twenty-four hour deli. Clearly she was the shot caller. Adorned in an expensive looking leather jacket laced with fur, Sabrina attempted to hide her face behind sun glasses and a hoodie.

"Wait in the car," both Rayne and Bernadette said simultaneously to Angel.

They both looked at each other keenly knowing the area wasn't a place for Angel.

"Let's see if Sabrina wants to go some place less grimy," Bernadette said as they hopped out the car.

"Grimy...? This your old hood." Rayne laughed.

"The key word is old Rayne; I ain't into this street shit anymore."

There was no need for Rayne to say anything additional. Bernadette was right, she figured. Rayne wasn't quite sure about the sort of shit she was still into.

fifteen

She eyed them keenly as they walked across the street towards her. Sabrina was very street wise and cautious. She was surprised to see Bernadette in the neighborhood, especially at this time. Sabrina hadn't seen much of Bernadette once they were released from prison. They had suffered serious injuries. Sabrina had lived with her mother just long enough to recover. She had nothing else to do but go back to the streets. Another hustler was posted up at the corner Trevor and the girls used to own. He was a small drug dealing hoodlum who had come up while they were serving time.

Sabrina quickly got involved with him and slowly housed the streets right from under his nose. Sabrina was gangstress extraordinaire and still riding with the rep Trevor and her had made back in 1994. They were officially disbanded and out of

commission but no one had forgotten the Fatal Four. Everyone heard about what went down in Philly. No one was sure what really happened. Most assumed Sabrina played a major role.

She lowered the hood on her jacket and got a better look at her girls. Sabrina smiled. Rayne was wearing a nice leather coat and her boots looked spanking new.

Despite the clothes, Sabrina could easily see that Rayne had gained weight. She knew Rayne inside and out. Rayne was the closest thing she'd ever had to a sister. Rayne also had given her the reason to be angry at the whole damn world and made her ugly.

Sabrina subconsciously reached, touched the scar on her face. Her fingers traced the long scar and stopped. She silently chastised herself for doing that. Rayne wore the biggest smile. Sabrina frowned and hastily walked over to Rayne and Bernadette.

"When did they let you out of the funny farm?" She asked still frowning. "The people in the nut house must be crazy if they let your crazy ass out."

Sabrina was the only one who could call Rayne out her name without being knifed. Rayne laughed a bit then gave Sabrina a frown of her own before speaking.

"You were a silly ass bitch for taking the rap. They had no case."

"Hold up bitch. You weren't supposed to be in the crazy

house for as long as you was. I heard that you beat a bitch half to death and was fighting faculty. I didn't take the rap so you could just wind up serving a year anyway." Sabrina laughed when she saw the change on Rayne's face. "That's right I've been keeping track of you. I knew they were letting you out this week. I was wondering when you was gonna come back to the hood."

"You should have paid me a visit or written," Rayne said.

"Nah, you know the rules and besides I think the feds were keeping an eye on us." Sabrina hugged both Rayne and Bernadette. They huddled like they used to, except Dora Dean wasn't there. Now it was a triangle. Sabrina whispered, "They found Trevor's body."

Rayne was shocked. They had found Trevor's remains after all these years. Sabrina moved away from them when she saw one of her drug dealing associates walking over. She met the girl halfway and spoke to her. The girl walked off taking half the people standing on the corner with her.

"We gotta go somewhere and talk," Sabrina suggested.

"Good, let's go somewhere far from here," Bernadette added.

"Who is that in the BMW?" Sabrina asked sounding suspicious.

"My cousin Angel," Bernadette answered. "He's cool."

"Think he'll drive us to my place?" Sabrina asked.

Sabrina called a shabby house in Brownsville her home. She shared the place with a rapper with demo tapes and a dream. He worked but wasn't bringing in the type of money Sabrina did. They pulled up to the house and Rayne told them that she would meet them inside. She sat without saying anything for a long time. Angel was staring anxiously at her. She coolly examined him. Finally, Angel broke the silence.

"You're connected with your friends again," he said.

"Yeah, it feels good being with them. We are so different now. I don't know what the future holds for us."

Angel laughed. "Well, you should think about your life and future first."

Rayne looked deep into his soft brown eyes. She knew he wasn't lying.

"Kiss me Angel," she whispered hoarsely.

Angel seemed shocked. He took the longest time to respond.

"Listen Rayne," he began.

Angel reached for the hand closest to him. Rayne guided his hand to her face and rubbed it on her cheek. Rayne moved in. Angel met her halfway. He froze and Rayne kissed him lightly on his lips.

"I got Gladys. I love her Rayne. It was nice seeing you,"

he said.

"It was nice seeing you too Angel. I want more from you," Rayne said and attempted to kiss Angel again. This time he kissed her back. "I wanna see you tomorrow night. I'm gonna get a hotel and stay there until I'm out of money."

Rayne knew her sister was leaving the following night. She didn't want to live with Riley and her husband in Florida. She had her girls. She knew Sabrina and Bernadette would take care of her and help her get her life in order. She just didn't know which way her life was going.

"If you call me tomorrow, I'll know you wanna be with me, and you'll come over. We'll have a good time and that will be that. I can make you feel real good."

"I bet you can," Angel smiled.

Rayne hopped out the BMW and shut the door. It was still snowing. Sabrina had left the door unlocked. She walked inside thinking about whether Angel would call her and wondering if she was doing the right thing. Angel had a woman and was fixing to get married. Tomorrow she'd find out if he wanted some of her or not.

sixteen

The Fatal Four loved catching their victims off guard. The second spot rush they did, the mark was a Harlem big timer. Rayne was stripping at the time. She gave a lap dance to a man with so much gold, platinum and diamonds, Rayne just knew they had to get him.

This was a spur of the moment job that didn't involved Trevor. A week later, Dora Dean accompanied Rayne to the strip club. Money Making Earl always came to the club on Fridays. Dora went to the strip club and sat at the bar. Rayne description of the unsuspecting mark was on the money.

Dora pretended to be a stripper just finished with her set. She told Earl everything he wanted to hear and she asked the right questions. By the time his hand was in her panties, he had

told her all she needed to know. He bragged about what he had, displaying a fat knot of dough. Dora worked the seduction for his knot. Luring him with the name of a fake escort service, she promised to make him feel real good for three hundred dollars. He took her home. On the way she reeled him in with a sob story about being homeless. Money Making Earl was hooked thinking Dora was the victim. It was the other way around.

He drove a Lexus coupe. They knew the type of car he drove and where he lived. Sabrina tailed him home in Trevor's car a few days before. When he took Dora to his place, they didn't even have to follow him. Sabrina, Bernadette and Rayne were already parked across the street from his apartment building.

Rayne told Dora to make sure he had plenty to drink while he was at the club and not let him take a piss. Money Making Earl ran to the bathroom as soon as he entered his apartment.

"Come out and show me what you got, baby," she said and then placed a call to her girls.

She confirmed that he lived alone in whisper and unlocked the door. Sabrina and Bernadette were able to enter with no problems. He returned with his pants down and dick out, just what Dora wanted. He was expecting to find her butt naked on his bed but found two people at the bathroom door greeting him with guns and masks.

Dora shrieked and ran out the door. She joined Rayne who was downstairs waiting in the car. Sabrina and Bernadette forced Earl to give them everything that was worth something. The items included jewelry, cash, a laptop computer and a bottle of expensive champagne they found in the refrigerator. Then they tied him up to a chair, pistol-whipped him senseless and scrambled downstairs to the car and drove off.

"Oh yes!" Rayne shouted when she saw Sabrina rolling up. It was one of two things she craved at the moment. She sat next to Bernadette on a sofa in the living room. Sabrina sparked the blunt and took some pulls before passing it to Bernadette. Just smelling the weed made Rayne moist and horny.

"What were you saying about Trevor?" Bernadette asked after passing the blunt to Rayne.

"They found his body in that garbage dump we buried him in." Sabrina began. "I guess they are doing an investigation. They came up on the Ave and started asking questions. People must've snitched that we was always seen with him because when the agents asked me questions they mentioned you, Dora and Rayne."

"Agents…?" Rayne asked before passing the blunt to Sabrina. "As in FBI agents…?"

"Yeah bitch. The heat is on. We did our thing real smooth. They ain't come back again but you never know."

"Damn!" Bernadette said.

"What now, girls...? Are we together again or what?" Sabrina asked.

Bernadette immediately shook her head. Rayne shrugged her shoulders.

"I don't know where I am right now. All I know is that I don't wanna go to jail and I need to start thinking about my future. I gotta get a job or something." Rayne said.

"You ain't gotta get a job, bitch. I got you. I got the hood locked down. Come work with me and we can get back to doing what we do best." Sabrina was looking at Rayne but then leered at Bernadette. "You acting like you finished with us."

"I'm not finished with y'all. You're my girls for life. I'm just through with all the street shit. I'm done Sabrina. I just wanna move on." Bernadette was wearing the most serious look she could muster.

"We got unfinished business to take care of," Sabrina said looking at Rayne. "We gotta get at Steve Stunner."

Bernadette laughed in Sabrina's face. Rayne was hogging the weed. She eventually passed the blunt to Sabrina. Rayne's head was spinning with delight. She was high and loving the feel. She watched Bernadette and Sabrina's silent standoff.

"We don't gotta get at nobody. What we gotta do is move on," Bernadette worded.

"Nah bitch," Sabrina snapped before inhaling the blunt.

She exhaled and then rose from her perch on the loveseat. "I ain't gonna let him get away with what he did to our girl and neither are you. It's us and we gonna go back to Philly, find that nigga and smoke his ass. Pure and simple," Sabrina smiled, assuming things were finalized.

Bernadette got up off the couch and stood face to face with Sabrina.

"You and Rayne can do what y'all want but I'm finished," Bernadette said reaching for her coat. "I'm leaving."

"Nah bitch," Sabrina barked, grabbing her arm before Bernadette could take the first step. "You ain't finished. Once you're in, only death can take you out."

Bernadette shook off Sabrina. "Listen to yourself. Grow up Sabrina. The Fatal Four is dead…died right along with Dora Dean, died when you shot Trevor in the head."

Bernadette had her fists balled up. Sabrina seemed ready to throw a punch at any moment.

"Everyone needs to just relax," Rayne said to both of them. She got up off the couch and got between the two of them. "I wanna get at Steve Stunner. I wanna kill him for what he did to Dora. I ain't sure if I wanna live the life I was living before though." Rayne focused on Sabrina. "We can't spend the rest of our lives robbing drug dealers and shit. I wanna get more out of life. I don't know what I wanna do but I know I don't wanna wind up back in jail. And I don't wanna get shot at."

"You two are a bunch of punk ass bitches. You two ain't really done any real time. None of us did." Sabrina took another long pull on the blunt. "We owe it to Dora to get at Steve Stunner. I ain't gonna go down to Philly and take all the weight myself. We started this shit together. We gonna end this shit together."

"It ain't never gonna end, Sabrina. It's only gonna end with us really doing some jail time or all of us winding up like Dora." Bernadette stated and started walking towards the door.

"You ain't going nowhere dyke-bitch. No one is leaving till we get this shit straight," Sabrina said grabbing Bernadette's shoulder.

Bernadette wasn't accustomed to being hindered. Sabrina riled something in her.

"Get your hands off of me bitch!" She warned Sabrina. "This ain't back in the days when I'd just do what Trevor said. You were never our leader. When Trevor died we were all out for ourselves."

Sabrina put a firmer hold on Bernadette's shoulder.

"Let go of me," Bernadette's voice thundered.

"I took over when I shot that nigga in the head. If you got a problem with that show it with more than words. If not get your dyke-ass back on the fucking couch and play your position."

It seemed like Bernadette was headed back to the living room. She never reached the couch. She turned around and swung a fist. The punch seemed like it traveled in slow motion connecting with Sabrina's jaw snapping her back.

Sabrina legs went wobbly. Rayne tried to steady her. Bernadette looked as if she was about to slug Sabrina again. She didn't. Bernadette just looked at her, shaking her head. She looked into Rayne's eyes with sympathy.

"Sorry Rayne," she said then walked out the door.

seventeen

Sabrina gathered herself and ran into the living room, pulling out a pistol from under the couch, she screamed.

"I'm gonna kill that bitch!"

Rayne quickly jumped on Sabrina and wrestled her to the floor. They rolled around for a minute. Rayne held Sabrina's gun hand. Sabrina pushed Rayne's face back in a vain attempt to get away.

"Get off of me Rayne! Don't make me shoot you!" Sabrina warned in between her huffing and puffing.

"Put down that thing and I'll let you go." Rayne said while tussling with Sabrina.

"Put down the gun Sabrina." Rayne yelled.

They continued struggling for a minute. Sabrina was way

bigger and stronger than Rayne but Rayne managed to wrestle Sabrina until she was on top of her. One of Rayne's hands was still clenching the hand that held the gun and her other was an elbow to Sabrina's throat.

"You're way stronger than me Sabrina. I know you can get me off of you. You don't wanna shoot Bernadette," Rayne said hoping that she was correct.

Slowly she got off of Sabrina.

Sabrina jumped up, cocked the gun and aimed it at Rayne. Then she tossed the gun right on the couch in frustration. Sabrina's anger and aggression had her body shaking. Rayne exhaled. Sabrina sat on the couch and put her head in her hands.

"What's wrong with that bitch?" Sabrina looked up at Rayne. She massaged her jaw. "That bitch hits like a man."

Rayne laughed, "Doesn't she though." Rayne got serious, "Sabrina I don't want us fighting n shit."

"Ain't nothing to fight about," Sabrina said getting up from the couch. "Bernadette is gonna be down with what we have to do." Sabrina gave Rayne an evil smile. "I ain't taking no for an answer. The Fatal Four is life or death. If she doesn't think so, I'll explain it to her the same way I explained it to Trevor." Sabrina's aggression was evident. Rayne didn't like what Sabrina said one bit.

When Sabrina had settled down she and Rayne began to chitchat. They reminisced about the old times, the good and the bad. They spoke about the future. Rayne assured Sabrina that she didn't want a life of crime anymore. Sabrina spoke of getting back at Steve Stunner.

"After that you could do whatever you want," Sabrina said.

Rayne wanted to avenge Dora's death and didn't press the issue. Rayne loved Sabrina and for the rest of the night they talked, laughed and joked around like there were no other issues. In the wee hours of the morning, Rayne was tired.

Sabrina was too. She was talking about getting back to the streets to check on her money. Rayne knew it was time to leave and asked Sabrina to call her a cab.

"Where are you going?" Sabrina asked.

"I'm going back to my sister's hotel room. She's going back to Florida today and I wanna spend some time with her before she leaves."

"What are you gonna do afterwards?" Sabrina probed.

"I'm not sure yet," Rayne said with honesty. "I ain't going back to the Bronx. I ain't staying with my mother n shit."

Sabrina reached inside her pocket and pulled out a roll of money. She gave two one hundred dollar bills to Rayne.

"Here's a little something to hold you down. Drugs and pimping ain't like it used to be Rayne. I'm like doing shit by myself. I'm glad you're back. Now shit can really pop off," She called Rayne a cab.

Rayne didn't say anything else. As soon as the cab came she hopped inside.

"Call me Rayne"

"I'm gonna do that Sabrina. I'm gonna call you."

Rayne was so tired when she'd got back to her sister's hotel room. She went straight to bed. When she awoke Riley, was getting ready to leave.

"I wanted to spend some time with you before you left." Rayne said with disappointment.

"You were sleeping so well Rayne, I didn't wanna disturb you. The offer is still open. If things don't work out for you in New York, you come to Florida."

"Ok," Rayne said and gave her sister a kiss on the cheek and a long hug. "I'm gonna call you all the time. I'll visit."

"This room is yours till the end of the week."

"Damn big sis, thank you."

Rayne wanted to cry. She needed to take her medication and was losing control of herself. Rayne was too hard to be crying over the way her sister was treating her. Her sister was always kind to her. Riley had all her bags and was set to go. Her flight was two hours away. Rayne walked with Riley downstairs and watched until her cab was completely out of sight. She went back upstairs.

Pangs of hunger tore through her making her think of room service. She thought about how expensive that might be. It was one in the afternoon, time for lunch. She was in Times Square where there were millions of places to eat. She had enough money to do whatever she wanted. She decided she wanted to eat in a very nice restaurant.

Rayne took a very long and exhilarating shower and dolled up. She was looking fine. She liked how she was feeling. Spending close to a year in the mental institution had mellowed and matured her. She took her medication before leaving the hotel.

Downstairs she asked the door man if he knew of any good restaurants. The doorman gave her a tourist map with many places to eat and things to see. Rayne said, "I ain't no fucking tourist. Just let me know of a real nice restaurant. About four or five stars. I wanna eat at one of them."

The door man laughed and suggested a Japanese restaurant on 48th and Fifth Avenue. It wasn't a five star place but they had great food. Rayne said, "I ain't had no Japanese. Is it like Chinese n shit?"

"No, order the chicken teriyaki." He suggested, tilted his hat and opened the door for a very sexy, Rayne Avila.

seventeen

Rayne ate at a Japanese restaurant for the very first time and loved it. She had ordered the chicken teriyaki like the doorman suggested. Afterwards she went around Times Square window shopping. Rayne realized while she was walking around that she really hadn't been out much. She had been trapped in a perverse and uncommon world that Trevor created.

After three hours of window shopping, Rayne felt like doing nothing better than hang out with Sabrina. She called Sabrina on her cell phone.

"I'll see you in a couple of hours," she said.

"That's what I'm talking about," Sabrina said smiling at her phone. "My bitch is back!"

Rayne wasn't sure about that. All she knew was that she

had nothing else to do. She walked into the train station and saw an ad for CUNY colleges. The thought of school hit her again. She read the number and stored it in her cell phone. She had to get her GED first. Rayne hated herself for not staying in school.

Men kept glancing at her while she was on the train. Kissing Angel replayed in her mind. He might not call back. Maybe he wasn't interested. She wondered. She looked at a couple of the men who were watching her. She wasn't sure of what to do? The only man she'd dealt with was Trevor. She didn't know how to approach men and had no idea of what to look for in a man.

Angel was different. She'd known Angel since she was a little girl. She wanted Angel. That was that. Rayne rode the train to her stop. She got off and exited the station. Above ground, she was in her old hood again.

Memories resurfaced. She didn't dwell on any of them for long. Rayne walked three blocks. She started smiling when she saw Sabrina standing next to a mail box.

One memory stood out above all the others. Trevor was having problems with a rival drug dealer. The dude was hustling his product three blocks away and was in a good position because crack-heads and dope-fiends generally moved past him before they reached Trevor and Rayne. Crack heads and dope fiends were generally not loyal. The dude was selling two for five's and twenties for ten. It was incredible. Trevor was losing money so he let the Fatal Four loose.

It wasn't a spot rushing situation. They went on a diplomatic mission that wound up being straight beating a dealer's ass. Trevor told them to have words with him. He didn't want the guy so close. Trevor was very reasonable but often enough reasoning wasn't enough. Sabrina wasn't very reasonable. That day they walked down the block she had other plans.

"I don't think we even need to say shit," Sabrina told the girls. "What's there to say? He knows he's fucking with business and the nigga ain't shit. If he was shit he wouldn't have to be as close to our territory as he is."

Sabrina made perfect sense to Rayne and Dora. Bernadette was unsure.

"Trevor wouldn't have told us to give him a warning for nothing. The nigga must have some sort of connections or something. I think we should just do what Trevor told us," Bernadette suggested.

Bernadette was level headed and respected Trevor's guidance. Sabrina didn't take directions very well. Rayne did what she was told. Trevor had never led them in the wrong direction. They were spot rushing at least one drug dealer every other month. Nothing had ever gone wrong and they never had a situation in their hood that a couple of threats and warnings couldn't resolve.

"Fuck that!" Sabrina snapped at Bernadette and the others.

Dora was silent as usual. Bernadette eyed Sabrina. Sabrina

was doing all the talking. They walked over to the dude. Sabrina didn't say anything to the man, nothing that Trevor suggested. He was posted up near a liquor store. One of his workers had just done a hand to hand transaction. They were all shocked when Sabrina walked over to him and pulled out a gun. They didn't even know she was packing.

It happened real fast.

The dealer knew they were Trevor's bitches. He didn't find them threatening. Sabrina smacked the dealer across the face with the gun. She hit him but not hard enough to knock him out.

Everyone in the area reacted. He had two of his boys with him. They moved in on Sabrina and the rest of the Fatal Four. The crack heads in the area scattered. Sabrina beat the dealer down to the ground. Rayne pulled out her machete. Bernadette grabbed Rayne and held her at bay. Dora watched.

It became a bloody situation. Bernadette couldn't hold Rayne back for too long. She had to fight. Someone threw a punch at Bernadette. She took a slug in the face and gave the guy two of her own. Rayne sliced one of the guys in the face, right up under the neck. The guy had grabbed Rayne but after getting stabbed in the chest, he let her go. Bernadette punched the guy she was fighting in the face again. She continued punching him until he was on the ground and unable to get up. The guy who Rayne had sliced and stabbed took off running.

"Bitch ass nigga!" Dora yelled laughing. Her girls were so

thorough all she had to do was watch and laugh. She saw Sabrina still pistol whipping the dude. He was on his back. Sabrina was over him, holding dude by his shirt collar. His face was dripping with blood.

Bernadette placed her construction boot on the head of the guy she had beaten down.

"Stop it, Sabrina!" She yelled. "You might kill him." She looked at Rayne and said. "Don't you dare do more," she warned Rayne. Rayne was about to set out after the guy she sliced up. "You've done enough."

"Okay," Rayne barked. She kept the machete low and moved over towards Bernadette.

"I don't even think I gotta tell you anything." Sabrina told dude she'd just beat. "If you still wanna fuck around, Trevor will roll up on you. If his bitches are like this, imagine how he is."

Sabrina let go of his shirt. His head hit the concrete with a loud thud. The dealer moved his situation a couple of blocks further north of Trevor's location.

That was back then. Now Sabrina was walking proudly towards her.

"I knew you were gonna come back Rayne," Sabrina greeted and hugged her with a smile. It was cold outside. Rayne had her coat buttoned up to the top. Sabrina had a couple of her buttons left open and wasn't even wearing a sweater underneath. She was wearing a flimsy shirt that showed all her cleavage.

Sabrina was hot to death.

"What's hood out here?" Rayne asked with a smile.

It was the beginnings of winter and Sabrina was making sure her people were hustling the drugs. Rayne spotted two people she knew were Sabrina's workers. Both were young girls and were dressed as fly as Sabrina. Sabrina never used to be overly concerned about the clothes she wore. Now she was wearing styles that were straight off the runway. They had all changed so much in the shortest time. Rayne knew a year wasn't that long of a time.

"I'm gonna go back to school and get that GED then see about college." Rayne said.

"Good, good for you. Didn't I tell you that after we get Steve Stunner you can do whatever you want?" Sabrina laughed at her. "I want you to meet someone. Yo Pebbles," Sabrina yelled at one of the girls.

The cuter of the two walked over. She was dressed as fancy as Sabrina and smoking a cigarette.

"Pebbles, this is Rayne." Sabrina said it like she had spoke of Rayne often.

Pebbles looked at Rayne with her big eyes. The girl was really good looking but not Dora Dean sexy. Rayne saw a few similarities though. She looked at Sabrina with the blankest expression. Rayne wasn't stupid. She knew what Pebbles' role was going to be. Pebbles was a replacement for Dora Dean.

"I heard so much about you. You're like a legend in the hood, a hood legend." Pebbles said, her huge eyes glued on Rayne. "Sabrina told me all the stories. I wanna ride like y'all."

"Your name is Pebbles right?" Rayne asked. The girl nodded. "Pebbles you can ride all you wanna. Me, I wanna live. I want kids and a husband or some shit like that."

Sabrina laughed. "Get scarce," she told Pebbles. Sabrina kissed her passionately before the girl walked away. Rayne was flabbergasted.

Pebbles looked at Rayne afterwards with eyes that were inviting. Rayne waited until Pebbles was out of earshot before saying anything.

"Sabrina, you getting like Bernadette now?" Rayne asked still having trouble believing what she had just witnessed.

"I don't fuck around with men anymore, Rayne."

"Sabrina that shit ain't true, you live with a dude. You told me so," Rayne uttered a bit shocked.

"True, but that nigga is a bitch ass. I run shit. He eats my pussy and sometimes I feel the urge for dick. He does what I say." Sabrina gave Rayne an evil grin. "What you looking so surprised for? You and Dora Dean ate each other's pussies in St. Louis. She told me."

Rayne's cheeks got red. "We were working." Rayne started uncomfortably. "Remember the rules; anything goes when we're spot rushing."

"Right," Sabrina said. Sabrina watched Pebbles still walking further down the block. Sabrina looked over at the slender girl's ass. "I'm working right now."

"Damn!" Rayne blurted.

Sabrina turned back and leered. "Don't damn me. What the fuck you care whether I lick pussy or suck dick. We used to share a man together. I used to suck Trevor off right after he had his dick in you and you used to do the same." Sabrina smiled. "I used to enjoy sucking you off of him. You taste real good Rayne."

"Stop it!" Rayne screamed. Her cheeks got redder. She was more angry than embarrassed. "Don't get bold with me Sabrina. I ain't no punk."

"I know you ain't," Sabrina said with honesty. She touched the scar. "I know exactly what you're made of. I ain't gonna tease you no more. Rayne, Pebbles could be down. We gonna need two new members."

"Two new members...?" Rayne blurted. "If you're thinking of spot rushing again you can count me out."

"Nah, Rayne you gonna do at least one with us."

"Bernadette ain't gonna do no more street shit." Rayne reminded.

"Fuck Bernadette!" Sabrina snapped with more volume than she wanted. She grabbed Rayne roughly and pulled her closer so she could speak lower. "If that dyke wanna be out then she's out. Fuck her! I'm talking about you and me and two new members. We will remake the Fatal Four. We gonna do a run or two and then go and get Steve Stunner. We gonna get him for everything he got, do it right this time. Smoke his motherfucking ass."

"Sabrina I don't wanna spot rush anymore or anything else that's gonna get me in trouble. I wanna get Steve but only for Dora. I don't care about what he got or nothing like that. I would shoot or stab him right in front of a police precinct."

"That's what I'm talking about bitch," Sabrina added.

"No it ain't. You talking about something else, something I don't wanna be a part of. And without Bernadette it ain't no real Fatal Four. It don't matter who you put down or whatever." After she was finished speaking Rayne reached inside her coat pocket and fingered the little knife there. Sabrina had made her nervous. She looked as if she was going to jump on Rayne. She didn't.

After a while Sabrina said, "Let' go to my crib and smoke."

"I'm down for that," Rayne said with delight.

Sabrina signaled for Pebbles with a whistle.

"Get the car bitch," Sabrina ordered.

nineteen

They drove to Sabrina's home. Once inside the house all three of them sat in the living room. Sabrina gave Rayne a bag of weed and a couple of cigars to roll the weed in. "I'll be back," she said walking out.

Rayne split a cigar with one of her finger nails and dumped the guts inside a waste basket. While she rolled the weed Pebbles walked over to the stereo system in the living room.

Rap music started banging. Pebbles danced around the living room. Rayne watched her gyrating hips. She still had her coat on and took it off while she danced. Pebbles didn't stop with her coat. She took off the sweater she had underneath exposing a flimsy shirt.

Pebbles sat back on the couch and began massaging one

of her perky breast.

"Dancing be making me horny," she said.

Rayne shrugged her shoulder's. She was finished rolling the blunt and lit it. Rayne took a few pulls. Pebbles watched her lips and the smoke coming from her mouth. Rayne didn't like the way Pebbles was looking at her.

"You and Sabrina shared a man?" Pebbles asked.

Rayne didn't answer.

"Well, y'all can share me," Pebbles smiled flirtingly at her. "I like the way you look."

"Good for you Pebbles." Rayne said looking up at her with narrowed eyes. "I don't get down like that."

"You ever been with a girl, Rayne?" Pebbles asked moving closer to her. They were both on the couch. Rayne felt like getting up. "No one can eat your pussy like a girl can."

"You ever got the shit beat out of you? No one can beat the shit out of you like this girl." Rayne said with a deadly glare. "I beat the shit out of people who disrespect me. You need to know that."

It was clear that Rayne wasn't feeling Pebbles. She passed the blunt. Pebbles smoked weed like she was sucking dick. Rayne watched. Pebbles licked the side of the blunt before she put it between her lips. She took slow, long pulls and exhaled the smoke sending long gusts straight up in the air. She looked like she was really enjoying the weed. Rayne didn't blame her. She was already feeling the high.

Eventually Sabrina returned and sat down on the love seat. Pebbles walked over to her and sat down on the floor between her legs. Rayne realized Sabrina had changed clothing. She was wearing a skirt now. Rayne was pretty sure there weren't any panties underneath. She saw Pebbles rubbing on Sabrina's thighs and inching her hands up her skirt.

"Do you bitches want me to leave?" Rayne asked.

"You don't have to...you my girl for life."

Pebbles passed the blunt to Sabrina. She puffed, finished smoking and handed the blunt back to Pebbles. Pebbles crawled on her hands and knees over to Rayne and held the blunt up to her. Rayne reached for it and Pebbles playfully snatched it back.

Rayne could feel the high. Pebbles went between Rayne's legs, holding the blunt to her mouth so that she could take pulls. Rayne smoked from Pebbles hands. When she was done Pebbles crawled back to Sabrina.

"You bitches are crazy," Rayne said.

Rayne was horny but wasn't horny enough to mess around with Sabrina and Pebbles. She watched them. She didn't want to but did. Pebbles finished smoking, passed the blunt to Sabrina and stuck her head under the skirt between Sabrina's parted legs.

Sabrina opened her legs wider for Pebbles' head. She leaned into the love sea and closed her eyes. Rayne watched

Sabrina's legs twitching and eventually one of her legs went on Pebbles' shoulder. Rayne couldn't believe she was sitting there and watching her friend getting eaten. Pebbles stayed under the skirt until Sabrina moaned and sank further down in the love seat.

Sabrina put the blunt in an ashtray. Rayne sat and watched. Pebbles crawled to her again. Rayne's panties were damp. The temptation to allow Pebbles to do what she wanted to do dogged her. Pebbles got between Rayne's legs and rubbed her crotch. Rayne was hot and moist. The jeans she wore could not hide her excitement. Pebbles felt the heat between Rayne's legs and knew she was terribly aroused.

"Get off me bitch." Rayne said in a serious tone.

Pebbles looked up at her with sexy eyes. Weed smoke lingered. They were in a haze of freakiness and confusion. Rayne wasn't bemused. Pebbles saw the meanness on Rayne's face. Pebbles rose from her knees and sat on the couch. She was real close to Rayne but didn't touch her again.

"I know you ain't had nothing since you got out," Sabrina told Rayne from across the living room. "You want my boyfriend when he gets home. What you wanna do Rayne? I got you."

"I don't wanna do anything. I'm straight, thank you." Rayne said.

Rayne wanted to leave. Her cell phone went off. Rayne pulled it out of a pocket and looked. The number was Angel's.

Rayne smiled.

"Hello," she cooed sweetly to Angel.

"What time do you wanna see me?" He asked.

She was overjoyed and horny. Angel knew she wanted to have sex and had called. He was so silent, waiting for Rayne to answer. It took her about thirty seconds before she said anything.

"What time is it now?" She asked him.

"Six o'clock." She heard him say.

Damn! Time had flown by so quickly, Rayne thought.

"I'm at my friend's house in Brownsville, where you dropped me and Bernadette off. Can you come get me?"

"Sure." Angel told her. "I'll be there in about an hour."

"I can't wait," she told him then ended the connection.

"Who was that?" Sabrina asked suspiciously.

"That was dick," Rayne said. Then she laughed as loud as she ever did in her life.

twenty

It was really cold but Rayne anxiously waited outside Sabrina's house for Angel's BMW to show. She rushed to the car when it arrived. Rayne wanted to kiss Angel badly. She moved her face closer to kiss Angel. Angel received the kiss graciously and returned the affection. She loved the way his mouth and tongue felt. She loved the way he smelled and was revved up.

"Where are you staying?" Angel asked.

She told him the hotel her sister had stayed at, in the same room. He drove to the Times Square area and pulled his car into a parking facility. After he got the ticket for his car, they walked a block to the hotel.

While they were in the elevator going up to the room, there was a lot of eye contact but no verbal communication. Rayne

purposely unbuttoned her coat and arched her back so he could see her breasts. Rayne rarely wore bras and was proud of her thick nipples. They were hard. She was sure he saw them through her flimsy top.

Angel's eyes roamed all over her. She loved the way he was ogling her. He was giving her a look that said he couldn't wait to get inside her. There was something else in his eyes as well. Rayne figured it probably was doubt and guilt. Rayne didn't give a rat's ass. Instead she started searching for the card that opened the hotel room door.

When the elevator got to the floor, they walked out. Rayne rushed ahead to the door. She swiped the key card. The door beeped and Angel pushed it opened for Rayne.

"Thank you, Angel," She smiled.

She was getting used to a good man. She thought about how good Angel really was. He was about to cheat on his girl. Rayne started to wonder if he'd done it before or not. It didn't matter right now.

Rayne wanted badly to put her life in order. Having sex with a man fixing to marry a woman wasn't part of the plan. With that in mind, she led Angel right to bed. Her sister had left a bottle of wine in the fridge.

"Take off your coat and get comfortable man," she said then went to get the wine.

It was already uncorked. Rayne got two glasses and poured

wine. Angel took the glass and damn near gulped it down in one shot. He was nervous and so was Rayne. Neither of them said anything. She'd have to make the first move. Angel was about to pour himself another glass.

"Wait," Rayne said getting up from where she was sitting on the bed. She began taking her clothes off in such a way that enticed Angel. He watched with great interest. Rayne's cheeks were red. She hadn't done this in a very long time and it wasn't done as a job. She was doing it because she wanted to, she liked Angel.

She unbuttoned her shirt and let it fall right to the floor. Rayne rubbed her hands over her breasts playing with her nipples, all the while smiling at Angel.

"Come closer," she said flirtingly.

Angel did as told and went to the foot of the bed. Rayne got on the bed, straddling him with her thighs.

"Don't touch me," she whispered. "Not with your hands, just use your mouth on my nipples."

Angel did exactly what she told him to do. Rayne arched her back as far as it could extend. She closed her eyes. A soft moan escaped her when she felt his mouth nibbling. Angel bit her nipple at times and used his tongue in a flicking non-stop motion. Rayne began unbuttoning his shirt.

Once his shirt was off, she reached down to what was poking her right in the middle. They were close and she was

straddling him with her thighs tight. Rayne wanted Angel deep inside her right then and there but she also wanted to savor the moment.

Rayne unbuckled his belt, whirled it around and tossed it. Angel laughed.

"I didn't tell you to laugh." Rayne frowned.

Angel arched an eyebrow.

"Let's see if you laugh now." Rayne said before flipping all the way back, bending like a contortionist.

Angel saw clearly that Rayne was very flexible. Her hands hit the floor first, her legs left Angel's lap and was up in the air. She tumbled all the way over until she was on her hands and knees.

"Wow..." Angel breathed.

"Shut the fuck up!" Rayne warned.

She crawled on her hands and knees, the short distance back to the foot of the bed. Angel was about to get up. She put her hands on his legs preventing him. Then opened up his pants and unzipped the zipper. His dick sprung out.

He was so excited she saw a bubble of pre-ejaculation on the tip of his penis. Rayne got busy nastily licking it. She kissed the head of his penis.

"Take those pants off," she ordered.

She touched herself as she anxiously waited for him to sit again. When he did she deep throated his dick.

"Ah..." Angel hissed.

Rayne tried her best not to gag. She did in the beginning. It had been some time since she'd sucked some dick. She bathed his pulsing erection with saliva.

"Oh sh-shit..." Angel moaned louder.

Rayne wanted to laugh but she didn't wanna spoil the moment. She licked her lips and took a breath then went back down on Angel. He was a good size, not to big yet not really small. She liked this because she'd be able to really toss herself at him and still feel that nice stinging pain once he'd entered her.

Rayne was dripping from her pussy. While she sucked on Angel, she slipped out of her pants. Angel was moaning and panting. He wasn't used to a girl who really knew how to handle a dick. Rayne could tell. She liked that. It made her suck his dick even harder.

She leveled her tongue on the shaft of his dick and went down with her mouth. She sucked her cheeks in allowing her lips to fit snuggly on his dick. Rayne moved up and away from it but her mouth never completely let go of his dick. She knew how to suck and from the way he was moving, Angel would soon bust off. Rayne simmered it down. She didn't want Angel to cum just yet.

She continued to suck him off and finished getting out of her jeans. He didn't notice. All he noticed was her lips and her head going up and down. She let his penis out of her mouth and stood up. She sat beside him on the bed. They were both

completely naked. Angel had a slim but muscularly defined body. Rayne figured it was from working on car engines.

"Get that bottle of wine," she said. Angel reached over the side of the bed and grabbed it. Rayne lied on the bed and opened her legs wide. "Pour it on me...all over my toes, feet, ankles, and legs. Pour it on my pussy, my stomach, and my breasts and in my mouth."

Rayne reached down and stuck a finger in her vagina. She was so wet it slid all the way in. She moaned. Stunned by Rayne's sexual acts, Angel's eyes got wide as possible.

"Yeah Angel, I can get nasty." She smiled putting her finger in her mouth and tasting herself. "Pour that wine and then lick it all off of me."

Rayne closed her eyes, smiled and Angel got busy.

twenty-one

Angel rubbed her stomach while eating her pussy. He poured the wine on her pussy. She was ready to explode. When he stuck the tip of his tongue between her lips, Rayne winced from the electricity flowing though her. His tongue stroked her clitoris and the orgasm happened.

"Damn it! Yes-s-s...!" Rayne yelled.

She could tell that her scream of ecstasy made Angel feel like he was the man. He didn't stop licking her clitoris. Rayne couldn't take it. She reached a hand down and pushed his head away.

The bed was drenched in wine and her body was feeling sticky where he poured it. It got cold where he licked it off. It was a great feeling. Rayne grabbed him roughly by his curly hair and

pulled him till it hurt him. She pulled his face right up to hers and opened her mouth for a kiss.

"Wait," Angel said reaching for the bottle of wine. It was empty. "We ran out," he said.

"Fuck all that," she whispered. "Stick it in me," she ordered.

"I gotta get a condom," he said.

"Nah, I want it. You gotta give it to me. I want you now," she whispered. Angel didn't hesitate.

Rayne didn't really know what went on after that but she quickly felt another orgasm. It was like she was in outer space. Rayne opened her legs wider. Angel slipped inside. Angel let out a loud moan. Rayne twitched, her body shook.

She was so wet, Angel slid easily in and out of her. He started pumping faster and harder. He had to concentrate to prevent from coming too quick. Rayne began whimpering. It was the most beautiful music to Angel.

Rayne had another orgasm one minute after he'd stuck his dick in. That was all she needed. Sighing, she was beyond satisfied. Rayne knew Angel was enjoying her. He was kissing and licking her on the neck while he flexed up in her sexual portion. She moved with his body motion. Angel had been working on Rayne for about fifteen minutes.

She was zoning but she could tell he was about to cum. Everything about his movements changed, he was pumping inside her faster and more erratically. Rayne straddled him tighter. She clutched his midsection with her legs, her arms were wrapped around his neck. Rayne propped her ass up while he was inside of her and coached him to cum inside her with her ass elevated. Angel tried to move away. Rayne held him with her legs and pulled on his hair so hard, Angel felt like she had pulled some of his hair out. He let out the loudest moan. Rayne screamed with him. She let go of his hair and her nails raked his back. Angel let out another moan.

Rayne felt his dick drive javelin strong and up into her. Then he held his dick real still. Angel stopped resisting. He let it happen, let everything that was within him gush out and burst into her. It sounded like he was crying. He was whimpering. She could tell. Afterwards both were breathing heavy.

"Fucking yes," she whispered in Angel's ear, "fuck yes."

They laid there until his dick got small inside her and slipped out. They stayed there until she felt his semen trickle out of her opening. Rayne fell asleep. When she woke up it was the next morning. Angel was gone.

Rayne took a hot and soothing bath.

The bathroom had some milk bathing powder. She sprinkled some under the faucet while running the bath. It looked

like a bowl of milk. Rayne figured she was the cereal. She laughed and talked to herself. She immersed her body in the steaminess of the water and let out a long sigh. The bath was so good, she felt like she would have an orgasm.

Rayne thought about Angel and how it felt when he shot his load. She wasn't worried about getting pregnant. As far as she knew she couldn't get pregnant. Angel was clean and nice. She wasn't worried about STD's. Rayne was concerned with what would happen next. She wasn't sure about seeing a man but wanted to be caressed. She didn't want a man who had to sneak around. Rayne wanted Angel for herself. She wanted to see what he would get her for her birthday and the look on his face when she got him something he liked. Rayne wanted to know what he liked. There were many things she now craved that she never wanted before. She wanted to really live life with a real man.

She also wanted to avenge Dora Dean's death. Rayne thoughts turned to the Fatal Four, her girls. They'd go after Steve Stunner.

"Ain't no more Fatal Four..."

The words hung dry in the moistened air of the bathroom. The steam from the milky bath water sedated her yearning. Rayne yawned.

Although just waking, she felt exhausted and spent a few more minutes dozing.

"I gotta figure out what I'm gonna do with myself. I gotta

plan my life out and start meeting people who make me feel good like Angel. Sabrina makes me feel confused but I'm gonna need her help with Steve Stunner."

Rayne decided that it was important for her and Sabrina to murder Steve Stunner. Afterwards she would leave Sabrina alone and start her life over. She had no money but was sure Bernadette would hold her down. Rayne made a decision between Sabrina and Bernadette. She chose Bernadette.

She needed Sabrina to help her with Steve Stunner but she would need Bernadette afterwards. After Steve she could finally move on with her life. She would never be finished with the streets as long as she knew Steve Stunner was alive.

twenty-two

November went by and December presented itself to Rayne Avila. Wednesday December 15th, Bernadette and Rayne were gonna go to the cemetery to pay their respects to Trevor.

    The blaring of the television roused Rayne from a deep slumber. She had been living with Bernadette and her girlfriend for a couple of weeks. She was lying on the living room couch. Everyday at 5 o'clock in the morning Bernadette's girlfriend would get up and prepare for work. She would turn on the television to Good Day New York. Channel five blared loudly.

    Rayne yawned opening her eyes. Jenny Chen was looking at her. Jenny smiled. Rayne looked closely at her slanted eyes and round face with an inquisitive glare. Bernadette had a really intelligent and cute Asian as a gril friend.

"I'm sorry if I woke you," Jenny said.

"Its okay, Jenny, I'm sleeping on your damn couch all the time and always in your way. I should be apologizing." Rayne said getting into a sitting position.

Rayne was wearing a pink nightgown her sister had picked out the day they went shopping at Macys. It was a skimpy and ruffled Victoria Secrets number. Jenny couldn't stop staring at Rayne.

"You're Bernadette's buddy, Rayne. You can be here as long as you need to," Jenny told her.

She would always get up early, jog for about a half hour before she did other exercises in the house and then she would go to work. Jenny's body was lithe and tight. Jenny was on her way back to the bedroom. Bernadette and Jenny lived in a two bedroom apartment. Rayne had the guest room but was always falling asleep on the couch in the living room watching television. Sometimes she would doze off behind the computer desk in the living room.

Jenny introduced her to the internet. Rayne proved to be a fast learner and began meeting men on the net. She started looking for jobs and gathering information about schools. Rayne couldn't decide between the culinary arts or computers. She found many jobs on the internet for computer technicians and hotel restaurant cooks. There were many eateries looking for pastry chefs and short order cooks. She wanted to be one of them till something better presented itself.

Jenny was hardly ever home and Bernadette had few friends. Jenny loved Bernadette enough not to mind Rayne. In any event Rayne and Jenny used the internet to locate Trevor's mother. Rayne wasn't close to his mother but she'd been around the woman. Trevor always took Rayne to any family event they had. It was either Rayne or Sabrina. After Sabrina had gotten sliced in the face, she rarely went anywhere. Once the Fatal Four was formed, it was all about spot rushing to Sabrina.

Trevor's last name was Beverly. Rayne always called Trevor's mother Miss Bee because that was what she told Rayne to call her. After Jenny had helped Rayne find Miss Bee's phone number on the internet, Rayne called her the next morning and asked for Miss Bee.

"I haven't been called that name in a long time," Miss Bee said, surprised to hear it. "Who are you?" she asked.

"It's Rayne, Miss Bee. Do you remember me?" Rayne wasn't sure of the impact she'd left.

"Rayne...?" The woman uttered and then said, "My god! Where have you been?"

"Trevor's dead," Rayne said somberly.

"Yes, my son is gone. He died how he lived." She started telling Rayne the details. "He was reported missing. I told the authorities at times I ain't seen or heard from him months at a time. One year later, they called me and told me someone found

his body buried in some garbage dump in New Jersey. He was shot in the head Rayne. Someone murdered Trevor and put him there."

"Oh gosh...!" Rayne said as if she'd just heard about it.

Rayne wasn't feeling good about acting the way she was. She was there when Sabrina splattered his brain all over the place. She had to wash some of Trevor's blood and bits off her. "I'm sorry. Did you bury him?"

"Sure did." Miss Bee snapped then let out a laugh. "You know I had to bury his sorry ass. We all loved him. We knew it was gonna happen the way it did or he was gonna get thrown in prison for a long time. What about you Rayne? What about you and that other girl; the tall one, the one you cut in the face?"

"Miss Bee that's Sabrina, she's still around. I don't be doing any street shit no more. I'm about to go back to school. I've been studying for my GED on the internet and I'm gonna take the test in a couple of days."

"Good for you." Miss Bee told her. "You need to stop by for dinner sometime."

"Miss Bee, I wanna know where you buried Trevor. I wanna go see his grave. I wanna say things to him that I gotta be close to say."

"You know he can't hear you no more Rayne. I know you loved him. You was so young and so messed up. You don't gotta hold on to nothing."

"I know Miss Bee. Trevor was all I had at one point. I wanna go see him. I need to bury a lot of things in my life, my mother, my father, Trevor is one of them." Dora Dean was there too, Rayne thought. I'll bury her when Steve Stunner no longer exists.

Miss Bee gave Rayne the address to the cemetery in Long Island. Before leaving for work, Jenny gave Bernadette the keys to her car. Bernadette and Rayne used the internet to get the directions.

"Rayne don't expect me to be talking to a damn tombstone with you, girl." Bernadette said.

"Shit, bitch I just wanna go read his name off of it and sit in the dirt."

"Are we gonna get him flowers or something?" Bernadette asked.

"I guess we should. I ain't never been to no one's grave before. Trevor was crazy but he was my crazy Trevor and he took care of me. Shit, Bernadette I'm crazy. But I'm alive. He's dead. If I was dead, I'd like to think that he'd visit my grave."

"Rayne the nigga would've definitely done that. Trevor loved you. He told me." Bernadette laughed. "He was fucked up. But he wasn't nearly as fucked up as Sabrina. Trevor didn't deserve to die, even if he'd fucked Dora Dean. And you know damn well he didn't try to rape her. Dora was giving Trevor ass way before."

Bernadette grabbed Rayne's arm. They were both sitting on separate computer chairs, facing the flat screen monitor on the computer desk. It happened so suddenly that Rayne cried out in surprise.

"Say it, Rayne. Trevor had been fucking Dora Dean. Sabrina knew it way before. Why did Dora lie and say he was raping her? I know Trevor ain't have to rape no bitch."

"I don't wanna talk about it," Rayne said.

"Well, fine. Let's see if Trevor wants to talk about it later, let's see."

"Fuck you, Bernadette." Rayne snapped. "Sabrina is crazier than me. You know why she shot Trevor dead. It was supposed to be just me and her and not all of us."

"There was more to it than that, Rayne." Bernadette was getting really frustrated. "There had to be more to that shit."

"Trevor had gotten Dora pregnant." Rayne uttered. "Sabrina wasn't gonna let no baby of Trevor's come out of any other bitch. It was either Dora or Trevor. That's what it was, Bernadette."

"None of this makes a bit of sense," Bernadette yelled. "You and Sabrina weren't even fucking the nigga at the time. You guys stopped."

"We stopped because of Dora." Rayne swiveled the chair around so she didn't have to face her friend. "If Sabrina wouldn't have snapped…? I would have. I can't have kids and I wasn't gonna see no other woman have one by Trevor. Sabrina was one thing but Dora Dean was something else. I saw the way Trevor used to look at her. One of them had to go."

"That's bullshit Rayne." Bernadette knew Rayne was lying. "You tell me the real story. That or pack your things and get out of my house. All the shit we been though I gotta know what the fuck is what."

twenty-three

It was too much for Bernadette to absorb. Bernadette asked questions as they drove to the cemetery. Rayne answered in a subdued manner. The dyke was shocked at how crazy things were going on around her. She had no clues because she wasn't sleeping in the same bed like the others.

"I think Sabrina and Dora Dean were fucking around, Bernadette," Rayne said.

"No…?"

"Oh yes. The last time I saw Sabrina she had a girl's head between her legs." Rayne shook her head. "They kept it from me. They didn't want any of us to know."

"I don't believe this," Bernadette exasperated. "Dora and Sabrina were carpet munching each other. If they were, you

know who the bottom was?" Bernadette laughed. "So you were all fucking each other?"

"I never slept with Sabrina…" Rayne let it linger.

"But you and Dora did some lesbian shit in St. Louis. Imagine how Sabrina and Dora argued over Dora having her tongue on your pussy, like it mattered. You two were sleeping with Trevor at the same fucking time. He would do you then Sabrina or vice versa or whatever. You bitches were all over the place."

"You're really enjoying this, aren't you bitch? Enjoying it a little bit too much." Rayne snapped at her. "Sabrina and I had found out Dora and Trevor was sleeping with each other since we met her. I think Trevor and Dora were gonna take what they had to another level without us. Bernadette, me and Sabrina ain't stop sleeping with Trevor. It was Trevor who stopped sleeping with us. He wound up just sleeping with Dora. It was like Dora Dean became the head bitch. I think Sabrina was fucking around with Dora Dean just to stay in the picture. That was the reason she never told me about it. Sabrina screwed up Dora's head."

"Which wouldn't have been the hardest thing to do," Bernadette said.

"I don't think Trevor knew about Dora and Sabrina. Nobody knew about Dora and Sabrina. I was pushed aside. I was still gonna love Trevor regardless. Dora was pregnant. We knew it was Trevor's baby that was inside her. Sabrina had me going crazy over that. I guess I wasn't crazy enough to kill either one of them."

"Are you telling me Sabrina asked you to kill Dora or Trevor?"

"Yeah, she wanted me to kill Dora. I mean we always talked about killing Trevor but what bitch never wanted to kill her man."

"Sabrina is bad business, Rayne." Bernadette warned. "Leave her alone, stay away from her. You saw the way she shot Trevor. I saw the look in his eyes when Dora said that he raped her. I knew Dora was lying. I knew Trevor didn't deserve to die because of that."

"I know Trevor ain't rape Dora Dean. Dora was giving it up to him. She got pregnant and he wanted to run away with her." She uttered. "Every time a man got some of Dora they wanted to keep her. That bitch had to have had super pussy."

"You're right," Bernadette said laughing after the enlightenment. "Wasn't Dora supposed to stay out of the Philly spot rush in the beginning, until Sabrina murdered Trevor?"

"Yeah, Trevor was gonna make it a three person job, we ain't never done shit without all of us."

"Trevor had suggested you or Sabrina do the inside work. It's all making sense to me now. He didn't want niggas fucking Dora no more because he fell in love and she was pregnant. Dora's dead and so is Trevor. Only Sabrina can truly let us know shit but it don't matter, Rayne. We saw Sabrina shoot Trevor right in the head." Bernadette was driving and talking. Rayne wasn't

sure if they were going in the right direction but in another hour they were driving through the gates of a cemetery.

"Nothing was gonna go right after Trevor died."

"You mean after Trevor got murdered, Rayne. We never checked Sabrina on that Rayne, why? Who gave her the authority to just kill him? We all had a relationship with Trevor, especially you Rayne. Why ain't you smoke Sabrina?" Bernadette didn't wait for an answer. "I think the section is over this way. Bitch, get those directions out. Where is his plot?"

They found Trevor Beverly's plot, parked haphazardly just a few steps away from the small tombstone and hopped out of the car. Bernadette and Rayne walked to Trevor's final resting place. They were each thinking about Trevor. Rayne thought of the moments that led to his demise.

Rayne and Sabrina had just got back from grocery shopping. Bernadette was in the living room while Dora Dean and Trevor were in the bedroom. Trevor had called them all to the bedroom to discuss their new mark. They were about to do a guy from Philly named Steve Stunner dirty.

Sabrina didn't care much for Dora Dean. That's the way it was at the beginning. It was Sabrina and Rayne. They were inseparable. Dora was a completely different thing. The rule Sabrina and Rayne had when it came to Trevor fucking with anyone but them, was lethal. Rayne never knew how deadly it would be until Dora Dean got in the mix. One day, Sabrina had a conversation with Rayne leaving no doubt about the outcome.

"Trevor's fucking around with that bitch." Sabrina scowled.

"How do you know?" Rayne asked. "I ain't seen them messing around. Trevor knows the rules and if he is then he is,"

Their situation with Trevor was crazy. Rayne didn't care that Dora Dean was getting some from him.

"I'm gonna kill him," Sabrina said with venom. "I ain't gonna share Trevor with anyone besides you."

Rayne listened and watched her get angrier.

"They're sneaking around. I'm telling you, Rayne. First, Dora leaves and then Trevor is gone a few minutes after. They're together. I looked out the window once when Dora supposedly left. She was right downstairs waiting for him. Rayne I'm gonna kill one of them. They ain't right."

"What's right and what's wrong?" Rayne asked. Sabrina didn't answer. Rayne figured deep down inside, Sabrina didn't know either.

The next couple of weeks after were filled with Sabrina's constant complaining about Trevor and Dora Dean. A month later it was like she had no suspicions whatsoever. Sabrina wasn't overly friendly with Dora. Soon they became inseparable now. Rayne

didn't know what to think. She thought Sabrina and her were tight as hell, now Sabrina and Dora were tighter than anything.

Back then, nothing truly mattered to Rayne. All they did was plot and plan jobs. The Steve Stunner job was next. Steve was a very interesting mark because he was the first mark Trevor actually knew. He was a friend who lived in Philadelphia, Pennsylvania. Trevor expected the mission to be a cakewalk because Steve had met Dora. Sabrina was furious because it meant Dora and Trevor had been to Philly. She was heated about that.

"Steve thinks Dora is my bottom ho." He told them. "One of you will play the inside with Dora. She'll make the introduction to Steve and you're gonna get real close. He gotta couple of crack houses on the south side. It don't matter which spot we rush, Steve is raking in the dough."

"I don't like this," Sabrina started. She paused looking at each of them, starting with Dora and ending with Rayne. "Why it gotta be me or Rayne? Why can't Dora do the inside like always?" Sabrina huffed. "How come she met Steve? When did she meet him? Why ain't we met him?"

"What does it matter who goes inside? All of you have gone inside one time or another."

Trevor was right. With the exception of Bernadette, all of them had gone inside one time or another. They all knew what he was talking about. Rayne was curious why Trevor introduced Dora as his bottom ho. It was interesting that Trevor wanted them to spot rush a dealer he knew. Other than that Rayne didn't see anything wrong with the plan. Sabrina found everything strange.

"You're fucking around with Dora ain't you?" Sabrina asked.

Dora let out a weak laugh and right after she laughed Trevor laughed.

"Sabrina, this is another job. There's no need to get petty or personal over it. Remember the rules." Trevor reminded.

"Fuck the rules nigga! We got other rules, you been fucking them. You've been doing Dora Dean." Sabrina was always strapped. She reached behind her and pulled out a gun. She pointed it at Trevor as the others watched in horror.

"What you doing Sabrina?" Bernadette asked.

"Shut the fuck up, dyke bitch! This is between me, Trevor, Dora Dean and Rayne." Sabrina looked at Rayne. "Right Rayne...?"

Rayne didn't answer. Sabrina had told her a lot of things. Dora Dean was pregnant. Dora and Trevor were fucking around. Trevor had stopped sleeping with Sabrina and Rayne. Rayne wasn't sure, anything was possible.

"Are you fucking Dora Dean?" Rayne asked.

Rayne didn't know why Trevor didn't answer. She wasn't sure what his silence meant. She heard Sabrina.

"Damn it Rayne, are you that dumb."

Sabrina put the gun right to Trevor's forehead. "I told you

I'd kill your ass if you ever fucked around with Dora or any other bitch besides Rayne."

Trevor laughed and swatted the gun from his face with a wave of his hand.

"Don't you ever point a gun at me again unless you're gonna use it, bitch!" Trevor directed his attention to Rayne. "All of you are my girls. We all in this and ain't nobody bigger or smaller than anyone. All of you go out and do what you gotta do to make that money. All of you have fucked a nigga for the team. Spot rushing is what we do." Trevor laughed right in Sabrina's face. "Bitch if we ever rushed a female drug dealer I would be going inside or Bernadette, right Bernie?"

Bernadette smiled at Trevor. "No doubt..." She sang out.

"I told you to stay out if this," Sabrina said waving the gun at Bernadette.

"This ain't about a job, Trevor. This is about you betraying me and Rayne."

"Fuck you, *Scar Face*." Trevor teased Sabrina. "Rayne you don't give a fuck right? You know how I do. You know how I feel."

"I guess," Rayne answered.

"It was Trevor who forced himself on me, Sabrina. I would've never done it, if it wasn't for him," Dora said out of the blue.

Rayne didn't think about it then but now that she was in

the cemetery where Trevor was buried, her thoughts were more precise. Sabrina and Dora could've been intimate back then. Together they could've set up Trevor. What Dora Dean said made no sense then. It did now. Rayne was thinking clearly. It began to seem like something sinister.

"This is getting silly," Bernadette said getting up and walking out the room.

"I knew you two were fucking around. Trevor I told you if you ever fucked around I would kill you!" Sabrina yelled. The gun was between Trevor's eyes.

"Didn't I tell you not to point the gun in my face, bitch?" Trevor asked before laughing. He looked over at Dora. "Why are you lying? Did she get to you Dora?"

Rayne didn't really think about things then. It happened way too fast. Bernadette had left the room. Once Sabrina pulled the trigger, Bernadette ran back in. The gun was so loud.

Blood rushed from Trevor's head like lava from an erupting volcano. It splattered all over the bewildered Rayne. Sabrina and Dora wiped it from their faces. Bernadette ran into the room just in time to see Trevor's body falling lifelessly to the floor. That was that. Trevor was dead.

Rayne remembered Bernadette's scream and Dora dropping to her knees next to Trevor. Dora cried while holding one of his lifeless hands. The gun fell from Sabrina's grasp. It hit the floor, producing a loud clatter. Sabrina backed away from Trevor's

bloody mess. She walked to a window and looked out.

Rayne saw blood dripping through a crimson haze. It was as if nobody else was there except her and Trevor's body. Trevor's corpse was in the middle of the bedroom. Sabrina had hit him between the eyes from point blank range. There wasn't much left of his face. Sabrina shot and murdered Trevor. She did it inside the apartment where they slept, laughed, cried, plotted, planned and lived. Rayne was so sickened that she threw up whatever was inside her stomach. She couldn't stop looking at Trevor. Bernadette was talking and Dora was crying but she couldn't hear anything.

Dora Dean had turned the volume of the stereo system in the living room to its maximum level. That was really strange now that Rayne was thinking with a clear head. They were in the middle of a discussion about a spot rush. The music was so loud that Trevor had to tell Dora to turn it off. Right after he did, Sabrina started making accusations. The only person living who could provide any of the missing pieces to the puzzle was Sabrina.

twenty-four

The plan changed when Trevor was killed. They had wrapped his body up in a blanket and took him to a garbage dump Trevor told them about. They dug a hole and buried him. Then they filled the hole with dirt and garbage.

It was all about Dora Dean doing dirt on the inside. Sabrina thought up the plan and shared it with them.

"Now you contact Steve and tell him some dudes murdered Trevor over some drug debt. Now you go in like you need another drug dealer to support you. Let Steve know that you're ready to ride for him, Dora. That's how it's going down. Now I'm making the plans. I'm making the rules."

In the cemetery, Bernadette and Rayne spent a couple hours in the cold reflecting on the times they shared with Trevor

Beverly. They bought Trevor a huge arrangement of flowers and placed it at the head of his grave. The snow came down just before they left the cemetery.

Bernadette drove back in silence. There was nothing at all to say. Sabrina had murdered Trevor. Rayne didn't tell Bernadette that she suspected Dora Dean and Sabrina had planned on killing Trevor. It all seemed so strange.

Rayne decided it didn't matter anymore. She wasn't going to ask Sabrina anything. She would hunt Steve Stunner and murder him. Rayne wanted to keep her memories of Dora Dean the way they were. Rayne wanted to continue loving Dora Dean for who she was when she was alive, not who she was now. Rayne wasn't about to judge anyone. They were all part of something horrible back then. There was no longer a Fatal Four.

"We were named appropriately, Bernadette. The Fatal Four sounds like a group of villains," Rayne said, once they walked into the apartment.

"We were villains." Bernadette chuckled. "We were all in hell. Rayne, do you still wanna get at Steve Stunner. Even now after you made your peace with Trevor?"

"Did you make peace, Bernadette?" Rayne asked.

"I think I did, girl. I can move on without dwelling on shit. I'm gonna always think about Dora and Trevor. I'm gonna miss what we had, what we shared, what we all shared. I'm even gonna miss Sabrina. I have to move on."

"I can't move on yet." Rayne said firmly. "I gotta kill him first. I ain't like you Bernadette. I didn't change like you did. I'm still the same old Rayne. I still walk around with a knife and I still take my meds. It's gonna end for me when Steve is rotting."

"I'm sorry to hear that Rayne." Bernadette said and hugged Rayne. Rayne returned the affection. "I'm always gonna be here for you. You're gonna take your GED in a couple of days, right?"

"Yup, I've been studying. When I pass I'm gonna go to school for computers or cooking just like I told you."

"What makes you think Steve is still living, Rayne? What makes you even think you can just go to Philly and kill this dude?"

Rayne thought about the questions and couldn't find the answers.

"I'm gonna find him. Sabrina wants to get at him. I'm gonna spot rush one last time," she vowed.

Jenny Chen walked into the apartment. Rayne didn't mind speaking in front of her. Jenny loved to hear Bernadette and Rayne's war stories. They ordered Chinese food and sat at the small dining room table in the apartment. Jenny listened with interest as Rayne and Bernadette continued talking.

"Sabrina wants to do a spot rush, before we get at Steve. I'm gonna ask her about finding out where he is."

"He might not even be hustling anymore. So much can

happen in a year's time." Jenny said.

"That's true Jenny," Rayne agreed. "I'm gonna find him and kill him regardless. It doesn't have anything to do with robbing him. It just gotta do with me seeing him dead." Rayne looked at Bernadette. "I don't trust Sabrina anymore, Bernadette. I wish you could be watching over me, like back in the days."

"I can't Rayne. I don't want you to do shit. I think you should just give shit up. You should focus on your future. Fuck seeing Steve dead and running around with Sabrina."

"Yeah, you're right but…"

"Everything must come to an end, Rayne, even the Fatal Four."

Rayne knew it was true. She had Sabrina, Pebbles and whoever else Sabrina enlisted as members of the new Fatal Four. Rayne couldn't trust anyone besides her girls. Officially, she only had one girl left and that was Bernadette. Knowing what she knew, she realized that Sabrina shouldn't be trusted.

Rayne was smart enough to know that she was playing a very dangerous game. There was nothing pending at this time in her life. Steve Stunner stayed on her mind. She wanted him off her mind, once and for all.

The next couple of days, it was all about her GED. Rayne

kept in touch with Sabrina but didn't visit her. She told Sabrina she was down with getting at Steve Stunner. She agreed to do one last spot rush but wanted to find out where Steve Stunner was.

Sabrina already had information on dude. She told Rayne, Pebbles was originally from Philly and knew of Stunner. He was around and still selling drugs. He was still making moves and making a lot of money. What had gone down in Philly didn't knock his hustle in the least way. It was business as usual for Stunner.

twenty-five

A couple of days before Christmas, Rayne was feeling miserable. She decided to spend the holidays with Sabrina. Rayne had already taken her GED test. She had no confidence that she had passed. She anxiously waited for the results set to come at the beginning of the New Year. Rayne didn't have much money and no real means of obtaining any other than what Sabrina was giving her. She thought about going back to stripping. She really didn't want that. Sabrina had plans. She told Rayne they could do a spot rush Christmas Eve.

"Ain't no nigga gonna expect that," Pebbles said with excitement. "Ain't no nigga gonna expect getting got on Christmas motherfucking Eve." She laughed. Rayne wasn't too sure about

that.

The holiday season was also known as robbing season. Rayne kept most of her suspicions and opinions to herself. Sabrina seemed pleased that Rayne was around and even happier to be doing another spot rush. Robbing drug dealers was in their blood. The new Fatal Four consisted of Sabrina, Rayne, Pebbles and Samantha.

Samantha was an Oreo cookie, half black and half white. She seemed as gangsta as any Rayne been around. Rayne was suspicious of Pebbles, Samantha and Sabrina. The plan was simple. Rayne knew that the simple plans were always the best plans. It was going to be easy.

Pebbles was already inside. She was a well known ho' and the dude was throwing a huge Christmas Eve party. A lot of ballers and divas were gonna be around but the dude carried a heavy stack on him. Pebbles already knew where he kept his stash.

It was going to be a walk in the park.

"He already knows about me and Samantha," Pebbles told them. "The last party he threw at his crib showed me how easy it's gonna be to get him."

"How so…?" Rayne asked intrigued by Pebbles' confidence. "Why does it seem so simple?"

Both Pebbles and Samantha laughed.

"His parties are always the bomb, a lot of drugs and alcohol. He doesn't have niggas over his house long. Usually at three o'clock in the morning he kicks everyone out, everybody but me, Samantha and couple of other bitches. We go up to his room afterwards, watched porno flicks and sniff blow. He's always tempting us to do the nasty with each other and him for money. He's a selfish nigga."

"See how easy it sounds, Rayne? All we gotta do is make sure no other bitches are left in the house 'cept us. And we make sure he's as drunk and high as hell. The nigga sniffs coke like Tony Montana."

Rayne saw flaws in the plan.

"Sabrina most of the time we wear masks and rolled up on niggas afterwards so they won't know who was getting them. Hooey Jameson was an out of town rush. He didn't count and died."

"This nigga might as well die then." Sabrina snapped at Rayne. "Are you turning punk like Bernadette? I like the way shit's gonna go down. The nigga lives out in Queens. He ain't shit and no one is gonna know about shit."

"You're right, Sabrina. Everyone at the last party was so fucked up on coke and liquor. He kicked them out. Me and Samantha were at his house for two days afterwards and ain't no one drop by. He ain't even call nobody. We did his dick so good, he wasn't even thinking about hustling."

Samantha laughed. Rayne said nothing after that. She hoped things turned out alright. Pebbles had talked about Steve

Stunner. Rayne was more concerned about him than anything else. Pebbles knew a thing about Philly and more importantly she knew Steve.

All of a sudden Rayne felt nauseous and threw up right there on the concrete. Pebbles and Samantha laughed at Rayne. Just as soon as Rayne got herself together, she punched Pebbles in the face. Pebbles staggered back from Rayne's fist. She didn't go down. Rayne wasn't satisfied with just giving one punch. She pushed Pebbles to the ground.

"That's my bitch. My bitch is back!" Sabrina jumped around yelling.

Pebbles got back up quickly. There was a lot of moisture in her eyes and her fists were balled up. "You wanna get it poppin' bitch!" She yelled at Rayne then charged in, throwing punches.

It wasn't a fair fight. Rayne had been fighting all her life. The first punch she threw Rayne dodged. Rayne gave Pebbles two punches. Both hit Pebbles cute face and sent her reeling back to the ground. Pebbles began crawling back away from an advancing and angry Rayne. Pebbles started reaching inside her coat. Sabrina pulled out a gun and pointed it at Pebbles.

"She got you good Pebbles." Sabrina said with the gun aimed at her. "Leave it at that. I told you Rayne was that bitch. If you catch feelings, you'll catch bullets."

Pebbles got up off the ground, looked at Rayne and Sabrina then started to cry. Samantha eyed Rayne maliciously.

"Keep looking at me like that bitch," Rayne warned. "I'll make those eyes so swollen, all you gonna be able to do is hear and smell me." Rayne laughed.

"See bitches," Sabrina told them once the situation died down. "See what it's all about now. Fuck around with Rayne if you wanna. If you ain't a killer you better not," Sabrina said putting her gun away.

"You got that one," Pebbles told Rayne. "You got that, bitch."

Rayne was pregnant. It was crazy but she could feel her body was feeling different. She hadn't heard from Angel since their tryst at the hotel. Rayne didn't think she could get pregnant. She needed to go see about her body. In the meantime she shrugged it off.

The girls stayed on the block. Sabrina made good money that day and once they'd gone to her house she gave each girl their payment. Pebbles and Samantha were shocked when Sabrina gave Rayne more money then them. Rayne did no hand to hand serving. Pebbles was pissed.

Pebbles and Samantha were whispering about it to each other while sitting on Sabrina's bed. Sabrina's rapper boyfriend was in the room with them. He was sitting on the bed with them rolling a blunt and looking at Pebbles and Samantha like he'd fucked them before. He eyed Rayne sexually. Rayne ice-grilled him until he focused on the two hos' on the bed.

Sabrina was standing tall in her usual Wonder Woman stance. She didn't seem to care about her man. He moved his face over to Pebbles and kissed her lips. Rayne arched an eyebrow. Samantha went inside the dudes pants, fished out his dick and began stroking it. He leaned back after sparking the blunt. He took two long pulls and passed it to Rayne. She puffed and coughed. She tasted something other than weed inside the blunt. Rayne was sure.

Sabrina's eyes got really wide.

"Damn Rayne," she said apologetically. "Cocaine is in that shit. I forgot you don't get down." She looked over at her man. "You asshole...!" Sabrina snapped. "Roll a clean blunt motherfucker. Roll one just for Rayne."

Rayne was as pissed as hell. Even though she had taken her meds, she began seeing red. It quickly simmered.

Sabrina's man apologized, took the blunt from Rayne and gave it to Pebbles. Pebbles smoked. Rayne watched as Samantha started sucking his dick. She was in the middle of something crazy. It wouldn't have made a bit of difference if she'd gotten mad. Pebbles passed the blunt filled with weed and coke to Sabrina. Sabrina smoked. Sabrina was never into cocaine before. Sabrina had definitely changed.

Rayne was spending more time with Sabrina than with Bernadette and Jenny Chen. She knew she had to be close to Sabrina. They were planning to rush this dude from Queens.

Samantha mounted Sabrina's man right there on the bed and started riding him. They were fucking and Sabrina and Pebbles were watching the show. Rayne tried not to concentrate on what they were doing but couldn't help it. She was horny. She had already smoked a whole blunt for herself and was high as she'd ever been. If she wasn't high around them, she would've sliced the whole lot of them until the bedroom became a slaughter house.

Rayne didn't like Sabrina anymore but she still had love for her. She didn't even know Sabrina's man's name. She heard him moaning and watched him shooting a load in Samantha. By then Pebbles and Sabrina were kissing and playing with each other. Sabrina had given Rayne a whole room for herself. She left them where they were and went to her room.

The pull of the blunt laced with cocaine had her feeling funny, in a good and bad way. She was feeling numb down around her pussy and numbness in her head. She reached down unbuckled her jeans and started playing with herself. She massaged her clitoris and brushed a finger right upon the opening of her pussy lips until she almost came. It must have been the cocaine in the blunt. She wanted to call Angel but wasn't sure of what to say to him. There was a knock at Rayne's door.

The person walked in before she said anything. It was Pebbles. She quickly took her hands from inside her jeans.

"I just wanna say I ain't tripping over you beating me up,"

Pebbles said before hopping on the bed.

"Get off my bed, bitch," Rayne yelled.

Pebbles jumped off the bed. She moved close to where Rayne was laying and moved her face in close. "You are so good looking. Sabrina was always telling us shit about you. I was always thinking that ain't no one as gangsta as Sabrina on the planet."

"Ain't nothing all that special about being gangsta, bitch. I do what I gotta do." Rayne uttered with indifference.

"Can I eat your pussy?" Pebbles asked. "I wanna taste you."

Rayne reached for a knife she kept under the pillow. She had an urge to pull the knife out and stab Pebbles. Pebbles reminded her so much of Dora Dean. Rayne thought back to when Dora had convinced her to do the lesbian act when they were inside on Hooey Jameson in St. Louis.

"This nigga is so black, fat and nasty Rayne. I feel more comfortable doing you than doing him. He can't even make me cum." Dora had told her amongst other things.

The only man who had made Rayne have orgasms was Trevor and now Angel. Now Pebbles was between her legs with a very sticky, wet and experienced tongue. Rayne came shortly after Pebbles started.

When Rayne woke up the next morning she was cuddled up in bed with Pebbles. Rayne pushed her away and to the floor.

Pebbles jumped off the floor startled.

"Get the fuck out of here," Rayne said real easy. "If you ever come in here again, I'm gonna leave you a longer deeper scar than the one I left Sabrina."

twenty-six

Christmas Eve came and went with a successful spot rush. It was like taking candy from a baby. Pebbles played her part with Dora Dean seductiveness and ease. Sabrina, Rayne and Samantha had made sure the dealer's house was empty. They taunted and teased about what they could do to him as soon as everybody else was gone. By two in the morning, everyone except for one of his boys was shown the door.

Pebbles walked over to Rayne and said, "He must be giving his boy a Christmas present, one of us. One of us had better keep him company."

Rayne knew exactly what that meant.

"Tell Samantha to keep him in the living room." Rayne ordered. She wasn't about to fuck no one on a spot rush. Only

Trevor could make her a whore.

Samantha did her job and kept the other man downstairs. He was so drunk, not even Samantha's lip service could keep him up. Pebbles was upstairs working her charms on the mark. Rayne and Sabrina went up to the room. The mark was already on top and between Pebbles' legs, pounding the hell out of her pussy.

With each of his thrusts, her head banged against the wall. She was screaming loudly. The sound of Barry White pumped from a stereo in the room. He didn't hear Rayne and Sabrina creeping.

He had a hand around Pebbles' neck, choking her. He was stroking her long and beast like. Rayne could see Pebbles' face. She looked like she was suffocating. Sabrina took a step forward, gun in hand. Rayne grabbed her arm.

"Let that nigga cum first," Rayne whispered with an evil grin, visions of crimson dripped. "Yeah, let that nigga skeet the fuck off."

"You want it, huh bitch…? You want my juice in you…uh… ah?"

Sabrina moved up on the mark. Rayne grabbed her by the shoulder. Pebbles couldn't scream, his hands clenched tightly around her windpipe. She was finally able to breathe when he shot his load and released his grasp on her neck.

She was coughing and trying to get him off her. The nigga was still digging hard inside her pussy.

"Damn!" he exhaled loudly. "I think I made you bleed bitch."

"You, you fucking asshole…! I'm gonna kill you! I warned you about doing it like that!"

Before the mark could say anything else, Sabrina put a bullet in the back of his head.

"Fuck!" Rayne yelled snatching the smoking gun out of Sabrina's hand. "Why the fuck you had to do that?" She exasperated.

"Damn nigga ain't even use a condom. He was raping me," Pebbles said while rolling off the bed. Her legs were weak and she fell.

"Bitch, that nigga ain't rape you. You said he was rough. You should've prepared yourself," Sabrina said with a cold voice.

"Why did you shoot him like that?" Rayne asked with the gun pointed to Sabrina's breasts.

"You didn't see what he was doing to Pebbles?" Sabrina asked ignoring the gun aimed at her. She looked at Pebbles. "Where is the cash and jewelry kept?"

Pebbles staggered to her feet. Rayne saw a thin line of blood trickling down her inner thigh. He had ripped Pebbles' immaculate weave apart and there were bruises on her neck. Rayne almost felt sorry for her. She looked at Sabrina with red eyes and all feelings of sympathy dissipated.

"You heard Sabrina," Rayne barked. "Where's the money

and all that jewelry?"

Pebbles responded by screaming like an animal. Rayne got closer and smacked her.

"Get yourself together. You wanna be gangsta right? What sort of ho' are you? You used to ho' on the street and now you can't take dick?"

"Rayne is right, bitch." Sabrina scolded Pebbles. Sabrina walked over to the stereo and turned down the volume. They were yelling without being aware of it. Things were a bit calmer. "Let's get the stash and get the fuck out of here. Look! There's a dead nigga here. We need to move fast." Sabrina snatched the gun from Rayne. "I gotta finish shit," she said walking out.

Rayne shook Pebbles.

"I'm fine bitch."

Pebbles went around the room and found the loosened plank of flooring. Pebbles pulled it up and lifted out a strong-box. There were three Ziploc bags filled with cocaine under the floor as well.

Two shots startled Rayne and Pebbles. The sound came from downstairs. Rayne whipped out the knife she had in a pocket and ran downstairs. She was stunned by what she saw when she got there. The dude Samantha had been servicing had been shot in the back of his dome-piece by Sabrina. Blood covered Samantha. Sabrina didn't give her a chance to push him off her.

Rayne was more scared of Sabrina than she'd ever been.

Sabrina was a mad woman. Rayne laughed hysterically. It was a clear sign that she had not taken her meds. She felt saner than Sabrina though. Sabrina had just killed two people. She didn't have to murder neither.

Sabrina held her hands up and calmed them before anyone could say or do anything.

They all took showers to wash off any DNA they had on them. They all carried a change of clothing. Samantha had gone outside and walked the four blocks to the vehicle. Sabrina took all their clothing and made a fire in the middle of the living room.

"Everything is going up in flames," Sabrina told no one.

"Bitch, you crazy," Rayne said with sincerity. "We're gonna do the Steve Stunner job and then I'm out of this."

"I don't wanna do this no more either," Pebbles said feebly. "My pussy hurts for real."

"Shut up bitch!" Sabrina snapped giving Rayne fierce, narrowed eyes.

Rayne returned the stare with even more intensity. There was a fire raging. Rayne and Sabrina coldly stared at each other. There were no words. Their eyes said nothing would ever be the same. The planets were aligned.

Rayne realized that she was carrying vengeance for Steve Stunner and more. Sabrina murdered Trevor as easily as she'd murdered the mark and his friend. Rayne truly loved Trevor. His death had to be avenged to make things right.

BRANDON McCALLA

twenty-seven

The events from Christmas morning hit the news hard. There were many miscreant people at the party and the authorities had no leads. No one would cooperate. Rayne had a suspicion that things would blow up in their faces. She figured some of the drug dealer's people might get at Pebbles and Samantha, eventually getting to Sabrina and herself.

The Fatal Four had always divided the spoils of their spot rushes evenly. The Christmas rush wasn't any different. Sabrina took all three Ziploc bags of coke and said, "When this shit is worked out on the street, I'll make sure everyone gets their share."

"Give my portion to Pebbles." Rayne told her while counting her share of the dough.

What Rayne said came as a shock to both Sabrina and

Pebbles.

"What the fuck would you wanna do that for?" Sabrina asked her suspicions on the rise.

"Consider it payment for Steve Stunner's whereabouts," Rayne answered directing her attention to Pebbles. "You said you know where he is, right?"

"Sure Rayne," Pebbles answered.

"You don't even gotta go inside that deep. You just tell me where he hangs out at. I'm gonna get him right where I see him." Rayne pledged.

"Nah bitch," Sabrina said rising from off the living room couch. "We gonna rush Steve Stunner and get him like we got those two niggas last night. It ain't all about you killing the nigga. That nigga got large money. I want some of that."

"Sabrina, this shit ain't about you. It's about me burying Dora."

"That bitch is already buried."

"I bet you ain't even go visit where she's buried. Bernadette did. I plan on doing so after all of this is done. You ain't visit Trevor either."

"Don't ever mention that nigga. I told you about that Rayne," Sabrina warned.

"Nah bitch, you told Dora Dean that and this new Dora Dean." Rayne looked over at Pebbles. "That's all you are bitch, just a bad replica of Dora Dean, a replacement. The nigga upstairs is a sad excuse for Trevor. Sabrina is living in a past that's over and done with. A past the bitch ruined."

Sabrina pulled out a pistol.

"Go ahead bitch," Rayne shouted. "Kill me and end shit. All things must come to an end. Bitch you just a spoiled brat. I wish I had the life you lived taking karate and ballet and shit." Rayne grabbed her coat and started towards the front door.

"Rayne you take another step and you're gonna get exactly what Trevor got."

Rayne turned around to face Sabrina.

"What did Trevor get but released from the madness. He stopped fucking with us because he knew shit had gotten crazy. He wanted to run off with Dora because she was gonna have his baby, something me and you could never provide for him. We were weak hos' who did whatever he told us, even sharing him. You got mad when you lost control." Rayne started yelling even louder. "Bitch you lost control the day your mother kicked you out the house. You lost control when you thought I'd be easy and I sliced your fucking face up. You had to live with a woman who was fucking your man, who scarred you for life." Rayne let out a mocking laugh. "I bet Trevor never said anything bad about me but he always said shit 'bout you." Rayne could tell from the way Sabrina was looking at her that she was right. "I knew it bitch. At night sometimes while you were snoring Trevor would whisper Scar Face in my ear. I'd laugh. I felt sorry for you because you actually

could've had a real life and you choose bullshit. Shoot me if you wanna bitch. Do it in the back of my head like you do everyone else. Do it when I don't expect it like the coward you are."

Sabrina lowered the gun. She went upstairs where her man was.

"Rayne," Pebbles called out.

"What bitch?" Rayne snapped already halfway out the door.

She was planning on going to Bernadette's and waiting until she got her GED results.

"What do you want?" Rayne sneered.

"I wanna help you get Stunner. I don't wanna be another Dora Dean. I wanna help you."

Rayne continued walking out the house.

New Year's Eve was uneventful for Rayne. 2000 went and 2001 came with her lounging in Jenny and Bernadette's living room watching the ball drop on television. Rayne had not been to the doctor or taken a pregnancy test. Her body was acting all crazy and she had gained some weight. She felt pregnant and hadn't gotten her period since being with Angel.

She didn't blame him. She hadn't told him to pull out. He never called. That made her pissed. She didn't really want to call him. She was responsible for this situation. Her whole life was one perfectly bad situation.

On January 3rd, Rayne received a piece of mail she had been waiting for. She had failed the GED test. Tears came silently. She really wanted to pass. Bernadette saw the disappointment on her face.

"Don't worry about a thing, Rayne. You can always take it over…" Bernadette tried consoling her.

"But I really wanted to go back to school." Rayne vigorously interrupted her.

Bernadette rubbed her hunched shoulders. Rayne shook her head defeated.

"If you want it, you gotta work for it."

"You're right, Bernadette. I'll do it again and study much harder for the test."

The next day Jenny Chen walked into the house with a copy of a GED test.

"It would be better if you study from this," Jenny said giving the copy to Rayne.

"Thanks for looking out," Rayne said.

"Not a problem," Jenny said.

An urge to see Sabrina hit Rayne. Over there, she was always so high she hardly worried about anything. Going back to Sabrina's wasn't a good idea. She hadn't seen or heard from her since Christmas. The last time she saw her, Sabrina pulled a gun

out on her.

Mid-morning, January 10th, Rayne's phone rang while she was studying. Jenny had given her a book on how to pass the GED test and Rayne was focused on it. Jenny seemed to be genuinely concerned about her future. She liked Jenny a lot. Bernadette was the most positive thing Rayne had going. She picked up the phone and realized the person on the other end was the most negative.

The caller id had Sabrina's name next to the number. Rayne answered and heard Pebbles' voice.

"Hello, is this Rayne?"

"Pebbles…" Rayne said a bit confused. "What do you want?"

"Rayne, Sabrina shot Wayne and is on the run…"

"What…? Who is Wayne?"

"The one who used to live with her…"

The wanna-be-rapper-boyfriend…? Rayne mused.

Sabrina was unraveling and moving lower than she had ever been.

"She just flipped out the other day. We were doing things with Wayne and she just went crazy. She pulled out a gun and shot at Samantha first and missed. She shot at me but hit Wayne instead. She shot him right in the chest and then ran out the house."

"Damn," Rayne uttered with sadness. "Where is she? Do

you know...?"

"I didn't know at first but I went to my aunt's house and Sabrina was in the hallway. She put a gun to my head and asked me where Steve Stunner lived. I told her. I thought she was gonna kill me. She said she'd let me live if I called you..."

"What did she want you to tell me...?"

"She wanted you to meet her out in Philly. She said, right where Dora Dean died. I don't know where that is. Do you...?"

"I know...When am I supposed to meet her there?"

"She didn't say. She just said that she was gonna be there and that she was gonna kill Steve before you did. She said she was gonna end shit. And that nothing was gonna end till she ended it."

"That bitch is wacko... She needs more medication than me. Pebbles, I gotta go."

"If you gonna go to Philly you gotta take me. I gotta see this end out..."

"Fuck you bitch!"

"No bitch, fuck you! Look at how you bitches are? I don't wanna end up like y'all. I wanna..."

Pebbles voice cracked and Rayne could hear her crying. Rayne hung up the telephone.

twenty-eight

Rayne convinced the reluctant Bernadette to accompany her. They were headed to where Dora Dean had died. It was a crack house that belonged to Steve Stunner. They wanted to go inside the kitchen where Bernadette and Dora Dean were ambushed.

Rayne had never seen where Stunner had murdered Dora Dean. She knew Dora was shot twice in the back of her head. She was unconscious, face down on the floor. Rayne wanted to see where Dora breathed her last breath.

"I'm doing this for you Rayne, not for Sabrina. I want you to put all of this shit behind you. None of this has to do with Stunner. Not Dora Dean, not even Trevor. It's about you right now. You need to get that through your head."

Rayne understood all that Bernadette had said. She

almost broke down crying in the car while they sped down the highway toward Philly. Rayne had a .32 revolver. Bernadette had another gun stashed.

"Let me carry both guns," Rayne said. "I don't want you doing any dirt. I'll take the weight if things don't work out."

"I ain't no punk-bitch! I'm smarter now that's all." Bernadette snapped, glancing at Pebbles through the rear view mirror. The girl was in the backseat of the car watching them. Bernadette changed the conversation. "Why is this bitch tagging along again?" She asked.

"Because she eats pussy real good," Rayne said looking back at Pebbles.

They all laughed. Rayne was feeling good about herself. It was strange because she didn't know what was ahead. All she knew was she wanted closure, wanted to bury all that haunted her. Rayne cared less and less about Stunner being alive or dead now. She wanted Sabrina stopped. She figured it could come down to her killing Sabrina, maybe Sabrina killing her.

"I owe Sabrina for murdering Trevor."

The words unconsciously escaped her lips. Bernadette and Pebbles heard her.

"Sabrina is crazy," Pebbles said.

"You don't owe Trevor anything, Rayne. The only person you owe is yourself. What do you think you owe yourself?" Bernadette asked.

"I think I owe myself some closure. I think Sabrina owes me some peace of mind."

Bernadette knitted her brow in confusion. She didn't know why Sabrina had told Rayne to meet her where Dora Dean died. She wasn't sure if Steve Stunner was still selling drugs in that place. Was someone else living there? Was the place abandoned and torn down? All she knew was that Sabrina was crazy. She couldn't let Rayne do this alone.

The Fatal Four were about to make one last ride. Rayne, Bernadette, Sabrina and the ghost of Dora Dean. They were on a quest to straighten things out. Once and for all, bury the past. The mission could bring the end to those who weren't already dead.

They arrived in Philly just before nine in the evening. At 9:45pm, they reached the south side and rolled up across the street from the house.

"I've gotta do something, so everyone stay in the car," Rayne said opening the car door.

"You ain't going in there all alone," Bernadette protested.

"No," Rayne started. "I gotta make a call first. I can't let y'all hear what I'm gonna say."

"Why didn't you just call this person before we left New

York or something?" Bernadette asked.

"Because I didn't know what to say, now I do."

Rayne walked a few steps away from the car. She couldn't stop looking at the house. It looked abandoned. There were boards nailed, blocking each window and the front door had a chain locked bolt that the Sheriff had placed there. It was probably being resold or renovated.

Rayne dialed Angel's number. He picked up just before his answering system did.

"Rayne…"

He said her name like he was really surprised. He didn't expect her to call him ever again.

"Yeah Angel, it's me."

"I haven't heard from you in a while. How've you been?"

You haven't heard from me because you ain't never bothered calling me, Rayne's thoughts pleaded. She said, "I've been pregnant that's how I've been."

"What…?" He uttered pretending he didn't hear.

"I'm pregnant. Nigga, don't even say some shit like it ain't yours. It is. I ain't been with no one in a year before you and ain't been with anyone after you."

"I wasn't gonna say that. How many months are you?" He asked her.

"Going on three, I think. I ain't seen no doctor or nothing yet." Rayne took a deep breath. "I'm really fucking pregnant. I thought I couldn't have children so I ain't gonna be cross at you or be hounding you. I just thought you should know about it."

Angel was silent.

"Are you there?"

"Yeah, yes I am..."

"I'm gonna keep the baby because this might be the only shot I get at one. I know you got your woman and you guys are gonna get married."

"We got married. I'm on my honeymoon right now. I really can't talk about this right now. Wait..."

"What are you doing?" Rayne asked.

"I'm going in the hallway. Gladys is in the bathroom taking a shower."

"What are you gonna do about me?" Rayne asked.

"I don't know. Rayne, I really don't know what to say or anything right now. I'm on my fucking honeymoon for Christ sakes."

"Do you care about any of this?" She asked.

Angel went silent for the longest moment. Before Rayne could hang up, he spoke.

"Of course, I care. I didn't contact you because I was scared, Rayne. I didn't want you to sway my emotions away from Gladys. Now I don't know what to say. I won't leave you high and dry though. If that's what you're thinking?"

Rayne exhaled. This could be the last time she spoke to

Angel for a number of reasons.

"I'm about to do something that might endanger my life..."

"What...?"

"Do you have any kids...?"

"We were planning on ah...working on that..."

Rayne knew exactly what he meant. They were doing it in the honeymoon suite. She wondered where they were but ended that as soon as it surfaced. "I just wanted to hear your voice. I wanted to know what you thought about me."

"I don't want you doing anything that will hurt you or the child you're carrying. Rayne I ain't a bad dude but damn..."

"I know you ain't but I'm a bad bitch," Rayne said cutting him off.

She closed the phone. Angel called her right back.

"I just wanted to see if you'd call me back and how soon?" Rayne spoke wearing a smile. "You don't have to worry about me, Angel. You're married now. Just know that you gotta mistress and a baby."

"Rayne don't do anything stupid. Just as soon as I get back, damn, I guess we gotta meet up. I'm not sure if I can keep this from my wife." Angel sounded saddened.

"You are a good guy, Angel. I'd advise you not to say anything. Don't call me, I'll call you."

Rayne completely shut her phone off this time. She heard

what she wanted to hear. She had a life inside of her and didn't want to do anything stupid. Angel was a good man. She had seduced him and it would be on her conscious, not his if anything bad happened. Rayne knew she had a conscious and a future now. She saw a couple of things in her future. Rayne smiled.

Rayne walked back to the car and handed the .32 to Pebbles.

"You ain't Dora Dean's replacement anymore. You're mine." Rayne laughed. "Everything is in your hands now. I ain't gonna do nothing."

"You don't wanna go after Steve Stunner?" Pebbles asked.

"I'm here to bury Dora and Sabrina. I'm gonna bury her while she's still alive. I'm getting closure." Rayne looked at Bernadette. "I'm pregnant, dyke."

"Shit, Jenny thought you were. By who…?" Bernadette's eyes widened. "No, don't tell me it's Angel's."

"Did you know he was on his honeymoon today?" Rayne asked.

"I didn't know if Angel getting married was gonna make you angry or not." Bernadette lowered her head. "Me and Jenny went to the wedding."

Rayne laughed. She wasn't mad at all. Not at Bernadette, not at Angel, she wasn't even angry at herself anymore. Rayne took a deep breath and slowly exhaled. They all became deathly quiet.

The house loomed a short distance away. On its front lawn, Bernadette had been hit by four bullets. She almost died. The whole situation flashed in front of her eyes.

"Coming here was a bad idea," Bernadette muttered.

"A major part of our lives was one bad idea. I'm here to end this old me and start the new one, just like you." Rayne took the first step towards the front door. "Come on bitches. This is the Fatal Four's final spot rush. Let's do the damn thing."

twenty-nine

The front door to the house was chained and locked.

"Sabrina isn't in there. If she is, she walked through the fucking wall like a damn ghost."

"Maybe there's a window in the back or something that ain't boarded up," Pebbles said.

They walked to the back of the house and found a window that wasn't boarded or nailed up. All the broken glass that might have been around was gone; Rayne could tell that people had been in and out of the place. Crack-heads, the homeless and possibly Sabrina, she thought.

"I'm not gonna crawl through that window," Bernadette said stepping back warily. It was pitch black inside the house. If Sabrina was in there she was in the dark.

"What are we gonna do then?" Rayne asked.

"You bitches are lame. I'll go in." Pebbles said moving towards the window.

Bernadette reached out and grabbed her by the shoulder with a strong hand.

"Lame or smart, little girl...? You decided that later. Don't decide it after you crawl in and some dope-fiend stabs you with a dirty needle out of fear or some stray dog bites a tit off. We don't know who or what is inside there." She looked over at Rayne. "I got some cable cutters in the trunk. I'm gonna get those and a couple of flashlights. We gonna walk right through the front door."

"What sort of bitch carries cable cutters and flashlights in the trunk of her car?" Pebbles asked.

"A bitch who is prepared," Rayne said. "You gotta be more careful."

Pebbles didn't say anything. She gave the window the once over and followed Rayne to the front of the house. Eventually Bernadette had come back with the cable cutters and three flashlights. Pebbles clicked her flashlight on. She had the bulb right up close to her eyes.

"Dammit! I blinded myself." She shrieked.

"Pipe down, bitch." Bernadette snapped thinking about something else. "Give me that gun. You are a poor replacement for anyone."

"Aw, come on," Pebbles whined. "Sabrina ain't even in here. She probably in New York and said what she did to fuck around."

"It's possible," Bernadette said holding her hand out for the gun. Pebbles reluctantly gave her the revolver.

Rayne waited for Bernadette to break through the chain lock. She pushed the door open. All three flashlights provided enough light. Rayne knew she shouldn't have told them she was pregnant. Bernadette and Pebbles halted her and walked inside the house first. Rayne followed behind. Bernadette fought through a few layers of cobwebs. Pebbles began coughing.

"It smells like piss and shit in here," she complained.

"Old shit and stale urine," Bernadette said.

Rayne shook her head. Old shit and stale urine meant whoever was loitering in here was gone. Suddenly a sound like heels on old creaking wood was heard. Then the house came alive with light.

"This place is haunted. What was that bitch's name again?" Pebbles yelled.

"Shut the fuck up!" Bernadette snapped.

"What was her name?" Pebbles asked looking around for a ghost. "The girl I replaced. She wants her position back. You can have it bitch."

Rayne laughed and stopped as quickly as she started. Rayne didn't realize how far they'd walked inside the house. She'd

never been inside but she knew from what Bernadette had told her that they were just about to walk to the hall that would lead to the kitchen. They were still in the front room. Rayne turned around before the rest of them did.

Bernadette should have remembered where the light switch was. Someone had turned the lights on. Pebbles' outburst had distracted her. She turned to see what Rayne was staring at.

Sabrina was at the front door. She wasn't even inside the house but outside somewhere waiting for them to arrive. She limped in carrying a 12 gauge shotgun aimed at them. Sabrina was injured.

"Sabrina what happened?" Rayne asked with more concern than she expected.

Sabrina looked like she'd been through hell and back. Her hair was a mess.

"I got you a present," she said. Sabrina noticed Pebbles. "What the fuck are you doing here?"

"Being scared," Pebbles told her honestly. "That's what."

Sabrina directed the shotgun and pulled the trigger. Both Bernadette and Rayne saw Pebbles body jerk back from the impact. It was amazing how Sabrina shot Pebbles from such a distance. Pebbles' body flew into a wall, fell on the dusty floor and was still.

Sabrina aimed the smoking shotgun at her girls.

"Both of you empty your pockets," she ordered.

"I ain't got shit on me," Bernadette lied.

Sabrina leaned the shotgun on the wall closest to her and pulled out a 9mm pistol.

"Let's see how good my aim is."

She took aim and shot Bernadette in the left arm.

"Sabrina no...!" Rayne yelled. "Don't do this." Rayne went inside one of Bernadette's pockets not caring if Sabrina was gonna shoot. Rayne tossed the gun she'd taken from Bernadette to the floor. "We ain't come here for this Sabrina. We came to help you."

"Help me for what, bitch?" Sabrina laughed. "How you gonna help me? You're the crazy one. I used to be the pretty one then you did this." Sabrina pointed to the scar on her face.

"You did that to yourself you demented...arrrghhh!"

Sabrina shot Bernadette in the left thigh. Bernadette went down kneeling with her good leg. "You fucking bitch!"

"Keep that mouth shut, Bernadette. Don't make my next shot be a head shot. Trevor used to take me out at night, out on the roof of the building and we used to shoot guns off. I always loved the sound a gun makes, shooting in the air used to get me off. Now, I like shooting people."

Rayne was perplexed and didn't know what to say. Sabrina had completely lost it. The scarred one grabbed the shotgun and started walking closer. She nudged her jaw towards the direction of the kitchen.

"This way Rayne, I have a present for you. You're all that matters now. You're the only one left."

Rayne immediately knew exactly what that meant. She made an attempt to stop it.

"Please no. Sabrina, please don't…"

Sabrina walked over to Bernadette knelt down and put the gun to her head. In a last ditch effort, Rayne rushed, dived down for the gun she'd tossed to the floor. Sabrina kicked it further away.

"Please, Sabrina. On everything we once shared…" Rayne pleaded with tears, looking up at her from the floor.

"Fuck this bitch, Rayne. What did Trevor used to call you…?" Bernadette's laughter came in pain. "Scar Face…" Sabrina pulled the trigger. It was point blank. Half of Bernadette's head tore from her body and burst in the air. The sound was clear to Rayne. She didn't hear nothing but the sound Bernadette's brains and blood made when they rained to the floor.

Bernadette's body fell completely to both knees and then to the ground head first. Sabrina slowly backed away from the pool of crimson liquid forming around what was left of Bernadette.

"She doesn't look like a man no more." Sabrina laughed. "She looks just like a headless bitch now."

"Why Sabrina…?" Rayne asked crawling over to Bernadette. She touched Bernadette. Her blood was still hot and it was thick and dripped all over Rayne's hands. She didn't care about nothing anymore. Bernadette was dead.

"You fucking Scar Face, bitch!" She yelled. "Kill me, bitch! Get it over with."

"Nah," Sabrina uttered with indifference. "In the kitchen," she urged.

Rayne didn't budge.

"I heard your phone conversation. You got a child in you. Are you that dumb Rayne? You wanna be so stubborn as to allow me to kill you while you got a child in you?"

Rayne broke down, pitifully crying. Sabrina was right. Rayne wasn't the same. Back then, she lived for nothing but her girls. None were left. Rayne had a life in her that was growing. It was the only future she had. How dumb was she to defy a person with a gun pointed at her head. This was a person who could end the life in her that had just started.

"That's right, bitch. Get up and start walking towards that kitchen. Me, you and Dora Dean gotta lot of catching up to do."

spot
rushers

thirty

Rayne walked into the kitchen and realized there was someone inside. She heard moaning, almost thought it was a ghost, but it wasn't. Not Dora Dean's ghost. The moan was that of a man.

Sabrina turned on the kitchen lights. Rayne could see. There was still a kitchen table and a couple of chairs. Two legs of the kitchen table were missing so it tilted to the side. Leaning against the circular part of the table was Steve Stunner.

"Oh my God…!" Rayne exclaimed.

Sabrina was nuts. Stunner's arms were outstretched around the perimeter of the tilted table like he had been crucified. Each hand was being held up by a knife that Sabrina had driven through his palms, nailing him to the table. There was so much

blood. Sabrina made a crown of thorns with a bandanna and a few syringes she'd found around the abandoned crack house. Rayne threw up her lunch.

"Surprise, Rayne," Sabrina said extending her arms out wide in gesture. "Surprise, Dora Dean." Sabrina put the shotgun right to Rayne's head and urged her to rise with it. "Here's the man of the hour, our sacrificial lamb Steve Stunner."

"Please," Steve begged. "Just let me go. I'll pay you."

"No!" Sabrina yelled. "Not until Rayne makes the sacrifice." Sabrina looked over at the kitchen sink. "Take a knife and plunge it into his heart. Get your revenge on him and let's go back to the way things were."

Rayne was dizzy and having difficulty standing. She felt like throwing up again. She was feeling nauseous and the smell of death engulfed the kitchen. Rayne felt the barrel of the shotgun at the back of her head. She was close to death, close enough to see the dead.

Her mind was playing tricks, confusing her. Dora Dean was where Steve Stunner was. She was nailed with knives right up on the circle of the table. She looked pale, was a corpse. Her eyes popped open and focused on Rayne.

"Hey bitch," Dora Dean uttered.

The words sounded as if she was alive. Her blood smeared, dry and caked up lips parted, opened wide. A black rat crawled right out of her mouth and scampered down her body unto the floor. Rayne knocked the shotgun away from the back of her head and moved further away from Steve Stunner.

She should've taken her medication. Rayne was confused. She wasn't sure if she was hallucinating. Had she seen Dora Dean? Was that Steve Stunner knifed up to the broken table looking like he was crucified.

"That was close Rayne," Sabrina said. "I almost shot you right then. You better not move again. You do, you and your baby die."

"What do you want from me?" Rayne yelled. "You've done enough. You've killed everyone."

"Everyone, except you," Sabrina said. "I got Steve Stunner here for you. Get a knife from the sink and plunge it in his heart."

"What then, huh? What do I do after that? What do you do, kill me?" Rayne asked.

"Things go back to the way they were, Rayne. Me and you can go somewhere, anywhere and start a new life together. We can get two more girls and do the damn thing. Start spot rushing again. We'll lead the crew together. Ain't no one gonna fuck with our heads anymore. Any nigga we fuck with, he gonna know the rules."

"Sabrina there ain't no us anymore. No spot rushing. No Fatal Four, nothing. You killed everyone. I don't even know why I came here. I'm just as crazy as you. I thought I needed closure

but there ain't gonna be none. You're the closure. You're killing anything that had any meaning to the both of us." Rayne forced her body to stop shaking.

"Where are you going, Rayne?" Sabrina asked with a very disturbed voice. "Don't take another step."

Rayne stopped moving towards the hall that lead out of the kitchen and turned around.

"I'm leaving, Sabrina. If you are gonna shoot me, shoot me in the back of my head."

"I told you to kill Steve Stunner, bitch. Go get a knife and do it. Didn't you tell me that was all you wanted?" Sabrina sounded demented. "You said that's what you wanted."

"I want Trevor, Dora Dean and Bernadette alive. I want to be with Angel. I wanna deliver this baby and name him or her. I wanna get my GED and go to college." Rayne was yelling at the top of her lungs. "I'm finished Sabrina! I ain't got no feelings for Steve Stunner. As soon as I got here, I buried those feelings. Stunner killed Dora Dean and could have killed any of us. We deserved to die because of the shit we did. We ain't deserved to get killed by you though."

Rayne began walking back towards Sabrina and Steve. Sabrina watched her confused. She saw what Rayne was readying to do.

"Stop...! I'm gonna have to hurt you Rayne."

Rayne started to yank the first knife out of Stunner's

palms. It was so deeply embedded in the wood of the table she had trouble removing the blade.

"Don't do it, Rayne." Sabrina warned. "I don't wanna hurt you but I'll kill you. We'll all be dead in this house."

"Maybe that's the way it was meant to be," Rayne yelled. She finally yanked one of the knives out. Steve screamed out a wail of anguish. His arm went limp and dangled loosely. Rayne started on his next hand.

"Bye, bye, Rayne!" Sabrina shouted.

A gun was fired.

It echoed throughout the house.

Sabrina's legs went jelly on her. She fell to her knees.

The gun went off again.

Pebbles crawled all the way to the middle of the living room and grabbed the gun Sabrina had kicked away from Rayne. She slowly crawled into the kitchen holding the gun and clutching a nasty wound on the side of her abdomen. The wound was not fatal but it felt like it was. Regardless of the pain Pebbles aimed and shot off two.

Sabrina dropped both guns and fell head first to the ground. Both bullets hit her. One went in her stomach, the other her chest.

The planets were aligned.

"Pebbles...!" Rayne screamed in surprise. "I thought you were dead."

"So did I," Pebbles said weakly. She was crawling on her hands and knees. She turned her body over so that she could be on her back. The gun dropped from feeble fingers. "Call an ambulance."

"Please call an ambulance," Steve Stunner said in pain.

"I should just leave you here to rot," Rayne said after she'd yanked the other knife from his hand. "I ain't though. It's over, right Steve?"

"I just wanna be left alone," Steve said. "I don't even know who you are. I don't know who that bitch was either." He said referring to Sabrina.

"It don't matter," Rayne said. "We ain't know who we were. I know who I am now. I'm a soon to be mother. If nothing else, I'm that bitch."

Pebbles managed to rise to a sitting position. "Bitch, fuck all of that philosophical stuff; help me up." She pleaded.

Rayne left Steve and walked over to Pebbles. She wasn't worried about Stunner. He didn't seem to be in any condition to do anything but bleed. Sabrina had shot him in the gut and impaled each of his hands with a knife. Rayne helped Pebbles up. Her wound looked really bad. Rayne went for the cell phone inside her pocket. Pebbles staggered right over to Sabrina's body.

"Call an ambulance and then call the morgue." She said after taking a better look at Sabrina. "That bitch was crazy." Pebbles bent to get a better look.

Sabrina popped up holding a pistol. She grabbed Pebbles by the collar.

Rayne turned around just as she went into her pocket to take out her phone. She had a knife inside that same pocket. It was a very small knife but it was sharp and the blade was thick instead of long. Rayne tossed the knife. She threw it more on instinct than anything else. The gun still went off. The knife entered Sabrina's forehead. The gun fell. Sabrina breathed in her last breath. She didn't get a chance to exhale. Sabrina tumbled to the floor. She was holding Pebbles. Pebbles went right down with her.

"Get this bitch off of me." Pebbles yelled after a while.

"I'm gonna call an ambulance," Rayne said sounding subdued. She tapped 911 with shaky fingers.

"Please help me…" she said once the operator came on. "Two people are severely injured and two are dead." Rayne looked at Steve Stunner.

"What's the address here?" She asked.

Steve Stunner was looking at the only other person living besides the one who just asked for the address and himself. She looked vaguely familiar. He had lost so much blood, and was still losing more. He heard more than one person mentioned the name Dora Dean. He remembered her. He'd killed her in this place that used to be one of his crack dens. He was forced to abandon it.

Steve was rushed to the hospital and some intensive medical procedures were done on him. He started remembering it all. There was a time he'd hit a man over the head with a bat then caught him again in the kitchen. He executed dude by putting two bullets in the back of his head. He would later find out it was Dora Dean wearing a ski mask. It was so bizarre. Someone called him a day before the incident and told him to be prepared for something.

"Who the fuck are you?" Steve said to the person on the phone and then he asked, "Be prepared for what?"

The person hung up the phone. To be on the safe side, Stunner warned his people to be on the lookout. His cautious reaction saved him from being killed that day. Stunner was tired of putting his life on the line. He was lying on the hospital bed with thoughts to stop hustling. Selling drugs was too dangerous.

BRANDON McCALLA

Now here's a word about the Gangstress Collection from the author, Brandon McCalla.

The Gangstress Collection is a five book collection of novellas that focus on strong, intelligent and daring female lead characters. They find themselves in very dangerously threatening and often enough sexually, electrifying situations.

This series is for those readers who are tired of the same old street fiction books with the same premise and chain of events. The Gangstress Collection is here to shock, humor, at times entice but above all entertain you. All the books are like snow flakes meaning no two are alike.

Don't expect the same thing!
UNO

GANGSTRESS
COLLECTION

BRANDON McCALLA

Gangirls

a preview

BOOK TWO

Bambi and Mink were inside the stolen sedan. They were crouched low in the backseats. They were there for close to 24 hours. Mink had to take a piss. Bambi told her to stop whining about her bladder and to hold it in till their task was complete.

Mink knew how to drive. Bambi was shocked. Mink wasn't lying. As soon as they stepped out HC headquarters and got inside the stolen sedan, she went under the steering wheel, rubbed two loose wires together. That started the car. She gave Bambi a little smile and drove.

"Where are we going?" She asked.

"We're going to Sky Jacker territory." Bambi told her. "We gonna park across the street from the barber shop. Then we're gonna get in the back of the car, watch them and wait."

That's exactly what they did.

Mink thought Bambi was crazy. Her plan didn't seem like a plan at all but it was a brilliant one. Bambi's mother once told her of how she and Reece had got the drop on a person by parking, hiding and waiting. "It's all about looking around real good and patience." Bambi told her. They were looking at the people across the street. Some were going, coming and hanging around the front of the shop. "If we keep looking we'll see which one we can run up on."

"Whose gonna do the shooting?" Mink asked with nervousness.

Both girls never killed a person. Both girls weren't anxious to do it. They really wanted to be apart of Homicide Central. They were gonna body a Sky Jacker regardless of how nervous and scared they were.

"I'm gonna do the shooting and you're gonna do the driving." Bambi told her partner with spunk. "I don't know how to drive."

Mink was glad to hear she didn't have to do the killing. She reached inside a coat pocket, pulled out the revolver and handed it to Bambi.

"You ever shot a gun." She asked.

"Yup, my mother took me to the roof top one day and let me shoot her gun. I shot off every bullet in it." Bambi boasted. What she said didn't reassure Mink. Still, it seemed like the best plan. It was the only plan they had. At least Bambi shot a gun off before. The first time Mink seen a gun up close was yesterday. She

Gangirls

took the gun from Burner quick but she was as scared as hell. She was scared as soon as she saw the thing.

While they were in the back of the sedan peeking out the window, they saw many things.

The barber shop never closed.

The gate went down the front of the building at night but the lights inside the shop were always on. People wearing sky blue clothing or bandanas around their heads or covering their faces were going in and out at all hours. It was a meeting place for the Sky Jackers.

Sometimes females would post up on the corner smoking cigarettes. They would wait outside till a dude walked out and then walk away with him. Bambi knew most if not all of those females were Sky Jacker girls. Sky Jacker girls were known for being hoes.

"Who we gonna murder?" Mink asked her the next morning.

It was the dead of winter and freezing outside. They had to keep the engine off. It was colder inside the car than it was outside. They wanted to get things done and over with but they wanted to find an easy person to get the drop on.

"You tell me." Bambi replied.

Mink had seen so many people around the barber shop. One person in particular seemed like the easiest person to murder. He looked young, possibly their age and he wore Sky Jacker colors.

He hadn't a jacket which meant he wasn't an elite member of the gang. It didn't matter. He had on a coat that was as blue as the sky and they saw him do the Sky Jacker handshake with someone. Both girls knew the guy was official. He'd been initiated in. Only an initiated gang member was allowed to do the handshake. He was affiliated with the Sky Jackers, killing him would make them members of HC.

They saw the dude more than they saw anybody else. Mink figured he was some sort of messenger or he was dealing dope. The Sky Jackers main source of income was heroin.

The guy seemed like the easiest person to get. He was always alone and they watched him walk three blocks down every time he came and left. Three blocks down was a project development. A project development infested with Sky Jackers. They were in the heart of Brownsville. Bambi knew once she rolled up on the dude and pulled the trigger anything was libel to happen. It wasn't going to stop her from doing the murder. Both girls were naively confident. They were filled with street lust, gangstress ideals and dreams.

They waited.

Another 4 or 5 hours passed them by. The day grudgingly turned into night. The guy once again walked inside the barber shop. He walked out the shop an hour later.
Bambi nudged Mink.

Mink crawled to the driver's seat and started the car. She

Gangirls

kept her body low. She made sure it would be hard to see her head and pulled out of the parking spot. Mink was a tall girl for 15 years old. She stood at 5 feet 7 already and was still growing.

No one paid the car any attention. Bambi saw every one in front of the barber shop. They were being about their business. Their mark was walking down the block. He was heading towards the projects.

Mink began driving in that direction.

All Bambi saw was the expression on Sky Blue's face. She pulled the trigger and popped two bullets in him. She couldn't believe it. She shot him, shot him twice.

Mink was so excited. They had done what they set out to do. She was driving the stolen sedan back to HC headquarters.

A police car whizzed past them. Mink saw the officer in the passenger side. He was looking. She wasn't sure what he thought. No sirens went off and the car didn't U turn in pursuit. Mink was only 15 but she was tall for her age. She looked older than she was. From a distance she looked like a grown woman.

"We did it." She told Bambi. "We in, we HC, we hood soldiers."

"He was nice looking." Bambi uttered. "He started crying

and reaching…"

Bambi wasn't sure if she killed him. All she knew was two bullets went in his stomach.

Mink drove at a slow pace, drove till he walked into the projects. She brought the car to a halt. Initially they wanted to pop from out the window, drive-by style. Bambi couldn't pull the trigger. Mink didn't fault her or call her a sucker or pussy. Mink was as scared as hell. She knew she wouldn't have gathered the nerve to pull the trigger either.

"I'm gonna follow him." Bambi told her.

Mink didn't say a word. She saw her girl tuck the 32 inside a coat pocket. Then she was out the car and walking behind dude.

He walked casually thought the projects. A few people were out and about. It was a dingy, dangerous development, swarming with Sky Jackers. Every person the dude encountered gave him the gang's hand gesture or shake. People were giving him a lot of respect. Bambi didn't understand. Everyone who was anybody in HC wore their jackets in their hood and this guy wasn't wearing one. Each gang did things in a different way.

No one gave Bambi more than a second glance. She was wearing all blue. Not sky blue, not Sky Jacker colors but a lot of people were wearing any sort of blue out of respect for the Jackers. She fit in well, looked like a typical hood rat.

The guy went straight thorough the courtyard to a building.

Gangirls

He had the keys to the door. Bambi was so lost in thought she bumped into him.

She was nervous.

She didn't want to get as close as she did but if the door closed she might not have been able to get inside. He turned, gave her narrow eyes. Bambi got a good look at his face. He was one of the cutest guys she had ever seen.

He smiled at her. She smiled back out of nervousness.

He smiled because she was attractive. Bambi knew she was good looking. She was the spitting image of her mother. She had the eyes of a fawn and the fullest lips. She had an Egyptians nose and the healthiest hair.

"Pardon me." Bambi uttered with a cracked voice.

She didn't know what else to say.

"Ladies first," he told her.

Bambi walked into the building.

The door closed.

She dared not turn around to see what he was doing. She knew he was behind her. She pressed the button for the elevator. She figured he was waiting for the elevator.

The elevator came.

The elevator opened.

Two dudes and a woman walked out.

The woman quickly rushed out of the building. That told Bambi much.

Bambi gasped.

Both dudes were Sky Jackers.

It was a miracle no one paid enough attention to look at her face. Her face was filled with fear.

"What is the deal Sky Blue?" One of the dudes asked him.

"Nothing Black Hawk," He worded. "I'm tired."

"Get some sleep baby bro. We got big business tomorrow."

Bambi heard the name Black Hawk being mentioned before. She wasn't sure where she heard it or who he was but she knew he was important. The guy she was about to murder was Sky Blue. She thought the name fit him well. It was a cute name and he was a cute guy. He was a guy she was about to kill. She saw both dudes eye her. As she was walking into the elevator she turned and saw one of them looking back. He was probably trying to get a look at her butt. Bambi wasn't sure. She was so nervous.

The elevator door closed.

"What floor?" Sky Blue asked her.

The sound of his voice made her jump. She didn't know how many floors the building had. She gathered her wits and looked at the buttons.

"10." She told him.

"That's my floor." He said, sounding a bit suspicious. "Who

Gangirls

are you going to see?"

"Maybe you," She sassed.

He laughed. His laughter was short lived.

"I never saw you around here before. Who do you know? How old are you?"

She was so scared. He was asking a lot of questions. He looked so young but he wasn't young. Bambi figured he was at least 20 if not older. His eyes told her he liked the way her face looked. Bambi was beautiful but he was suspicious. He never seen her around and wanted to know why.

A hand was in a coat pocket. She had a few fingers nervously tickling the handle of the revolver. All she had to do was pull the gun out and pull the trigger. He was so close she wouldn't have to aim the gun.

"Who do you know around here, girl?" He asked her again.

He gave her a more definitive look.

"Take that hand out of your pocket." He instructed.

Bambi pulled the gun out along with her hand.

His eyes got wide.

The elevator beeped...

It reached the 8th floor. By the time it reached 9 she had pulled the trigger twice. By the time the door opened on the 10th floor, Sky Blue was on the floor in the middle of a pool of blood. One bullet went in and out his stomach. The other went in the same area but stayed in his gut.

She wasn't sure if he was dead or not. She ran out the elevator and went to the staircase. She ran down 10 flights.

A few people were downstairs in the lobby.

She kept running till she was out the building.

She didn't look at anyone.

Mink had the engine running.

People were outside. Bambi didn't pay them any notice. Anyone could have reached out and grabbed her. She was looking ahead. She wasn't sure if she was holding the gun or if she dropped it. She wasn't about to think about anything but Mink and the getaway car.

Mink reached over and opened the passenger side door. When Bambi shut the door Mink peeled out.

"Did you do it?" Mink questioned. She had butterflies in her stomach.

"I shot him twice."

"Damn," Mink exasperated. "Double damn!"

Bambi looked down at her hand. Her fingers were still clutching the revolver; her coat was covered with blood. She put the smoking gun inside her coat pocket but couldn't take her fingers from around the handle. It was glued to her hand.

"I think you killed him. All that blood on you." Mink whispered.

Bambi started crying. "So do I," She sobbed. "I think I

Gangirls

killed him."

They parked around the corner from headquarters. After that, they walked to the door. Bambi was as silent as a mouse.

Mink banged on the front door.

Pretty Thug opened the door. He peeked outside, looked around the hood. He saw a few HC soldiers around. It was December 15th. It was cold outside. Snow started coming down in a flurry.

"You two," He worded with a frown. "What are you two doing here?"

Mink wasn't sure if she was allowed to speak to him or not. They were only allowed to talk to Boogie. They had passed their final test. She felt like she had the right to say something. Pretty Thug didn't seem like he was gonna let them inside. It was so cold out.

Mink was so excited she spoke to him. "Let us in." She said boldly. "We did it."

"Did what?" He asked.

"We killed a Sky Jacker," Was her response.

"Where's your proof?" He asked them.

Mink looked at Bambi. She didn't know they had to bring proof. She wasn't any where near Bambi when she did what she did. She wasn't sure if Bambi had done anything. She gave her a suspicious look.

Bambi was so silent. She pulled the revolver out of her

coat pocket and handed it to Pretty Thug. "I killed Sky Blue. I killed Black Hawk's baby brother."

"Holy shit, he blurted. He couldn't believe the words that came out of Bambi's mouth. Pretty Thug saw blood. It was all over the front of Bambi's coat. He was certain it wasn't her blood, "Inside now."

Once the girls were in Cujo walked over to them. Pretty Thug whispered something.

"Wow." Cujo could only say that. He took some time to think. "If you murdered Sky Blue, things are gonna get interesting." He told Pretty Thug. "Take them to the room." He looked at Bambi. "Take off that coat." He called Zero over. Zero was in the living room with Trixie. Trixie was a female he claimed. They were on the couch cuddling up. "Burn that coat and get rid of the car. Then go out and get the word on Sky Blue. I wanna know what is what."

"Right," Zero uttered, "Sky Blue" with some confusion. He was always confused.

"I stole that car." Mink spoke boldly.

"So what," Cujo snapped. "What ever you do ain't you no more, it's HC. Stealing that car was apart of the initiation. Any time something is done in a car, the car gets ditched." He wasn't sure why he was explaining anything. He gave her a longer look. Mink was young but she had long legs and a nice ass. Her face wasn't bad either. Cujo gave her a big smile. "I don't want you talking. Boogie is gonna be back soon."

Gangirls

With that being said, Pretty Thug led the girl up the stairs and to a room. The room had two beds in it, a few chairs, some other furniture and a small table. A television was in the room and a small clock radio. Pretty Thug left the room just as soon as he walked them inside.

It was Bambi and Mink.

"Did you kill him?" Mink asked.

"I shot him twice." Bambi said after a minute.

"That don't mean he's dead."

"How many bullets you gotta use to kill somebody?" Bambi snapped.

Mink naively said, "Maybe three instead of two or a hundred. I don't know."

"His name was Sky Blue." Bambi told her. "I heard him taking to Black Hawk. He called Sky Blue baby bro."

"I ain't ever heard of either of them. I ain't heard of none of them besides Air. Air is the leader of the Sky Jackers."

"I know." Bambi started crying again. "I killed him. I know I did."

"You had to kill him. How else was we gonna get in the gang so quick. Now we hood soldiers. We ain't initiation bitches no more. We ain't regular soldiers either. We hood soldiers. We get jackets and we can get HC tattoos if we wanna. I wanna tattoo right on one of my tits."

"I don't feel good." Bambi said and threw up.

"Oh shit!" Mink yelled.

Bambi threw up everything that was in her stomach on the floor. She fell to her hands and knees afterwards. "I killed somebody." She sobbed.

Mink went down to the floor beside her.

"It's ok," She said. She began rubbing Bambi's back. Mink kissed her on the forehead. "We need to clean this up." Mink wasn't sure if they could leave the room or not. She wasn't sure of anything. She wasn't even sure if Bambi killed the guy. She saw the blood on her coat. She knew Bambi had at least shot the dude. Bambi claimed to have shot him twice. Mink had to believe her. They were peas in a pod now. Mink had just met Bambi but she had faith in her. Bambi was Candace Lorraine's daughter. What was more thorough than that...?

"I got school tomorrow." Mink blurted absentmindedly. "Fuck school," She blurted directly afterwards. "I'm failing anyway."

Bambi said nothing. She was sitting on one of the beds. She was looking at the mess she put on the floor. She didn't know what to do. Mink went over to a chest of drawers and rummaged through some of the drawers. She found sheets and pillow cases. She used one of the pillow cases, cleaned the mess up. Bambi thanked her with a smile.

They waited.

Hours passed.

Gangirls

Mink gathered nerve and turned on the television. They watched a couple of shows. There was a knock at the door. Both girls said nothing. Eventually the door opened.

Boogie walked in.

He gave both girls angry eyes.

"I don't think you two understand what you did. Zero came back with the word." He looked at Bambi specifically. "The word spread like crack. You killed a Sky Jacker."

"We did it, me and Bambi both." Mink expressed with delight. "I drove the car. We done it together."

Boogie stifled her delight with a leer. "Be quiet bitch. You two did good but you done bad." He concentrated on Bambi. "Did anyone see you?" He asked her.

"See me what?" She uttered sheepishly.

"Kill Sky Blue."

"No one was around when I shot him."

"For our sake I hope no one was and no one finds out. If anybody points the finger at Homicide Central… killing an elite member of the Sky Jackers is gonna start a war."

Bambi and Mink couldn't believe what they were hearing. Sky Blue was an elite member. Bambi murdered a major member of the gang.

"You two are in, in a big way." Boogie smiled. "The ceremony is in two hours. We gotta do things quick. I got a job for you two just as soon as you're sworn in. If you gotta go home or something, do so. You two gotta have escorts if you leave."

"Why?" Mink asked.

"If anyone points you two out, you two are as good as dead. The Sky Jackers are nothing to mess with. I should kill Cujo for making you two…" Boogie hadn't anymore words. What was done was done.

Contact Brandon McCalla at *brandonmccalla@gmail.com*

BRANDON McCALLA

Brandon Dewitt McCalla was born in Brooklyn New York. He was always an intense reader starting with Marvel Comic books as a lad, but a copy of J.R.R Tolkien's The Lord of the Rings trilogy collecting dust on the book shelf in the living room was the true catalyst that set off the spark that world eventually make him an author. Once he graduated from high school and began his freshman of college he also began to write his first novel. He graduated with a bachelor's in the English arts and put his author endeavors aside to dabble in journalism and the music industry co owning his own record label for a short time and producing music. McCalla

considers him self more a horror and science fiction/fantasy writer than anything else. However, his first published novels Diamond Drought, Diamond Dynasty and Reign of the Pimp books 1,2 and 3 from an unspecified length book series called the Diamond Series is pure street/hip-hop fiction- an ode to the hip hop community and its music. He specifically wrote the gangsta soap opera for people who love the culture and want an entertaining and fast paced read. Something for the train when you're on it early in the morn; something to spark that day off before school, work or college... Brandon currently writes and holds the Editor in Chief hat for a number of early staged magazines and publications, i.b. Concept being the one he's the most focused on since his syndicated column Literary Hood was birthed their. Literary Hood is where he speaks candidly and explicitly on the urban literary circuit and does outstanding book reviews in his
Words of Art segment of the column.

[LITERALLY DOPE]

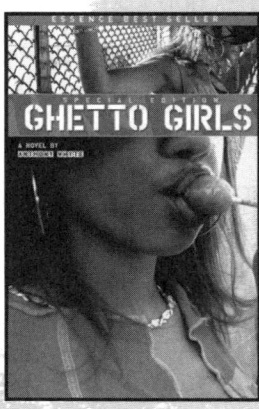

GHETTO GIRLS
AUTHOR // ANTHONY WHYTE
ISBN: 0975945319 // $14.95

GHETTO GIRLS TOO
AUTHOR // ANTHONY WHYTE
ISBN: 0975945300 // $14.95

GHETTO GIRLS 3: SOO HOOD
AUTHOR // ANTHONY WHYTE
ISBN: 0975945351 // $14.95

THE BLUE CIRCLE
AUTHOR // KEISHA SEIGNIOUS
ISBN: 0975945335 // $14.95

BOOTY CALL *69
AUTHOR // ERICK S GRAY
ISBN: 0975945343 // $14.95

IT CAN HAPPEN IN A MINUTE
AUTHOR // S.M. JOHNSON
ISBN: 0975945378 // $14.95

AUGUSTUS PUBLISHING

WHERE **HIP HOP LITERATURE** BEGINS...

Augustus Publishing exposes talented writers by bringing stories of unparalleled breadth, depth, and vision to the book market. We publish quality works of fiction in the category of **Hip Hop literature**.

Our stories express the widest possible range of the urban experience...

WOMAN'S CRY
AUTHOR // **VANESSA MARTIR**
ISBN: 0975945386 // $14.95

A GOOD DAY TO DIE
AUTHOR // **JAMES HENDRICKS**
ISBN: 0975945327 // $14.95

LIP STICK DIARIES
AUTHOR // **VARIOUS FEMALE AUTHORS**
ISBN: 0975945319 // $14.95

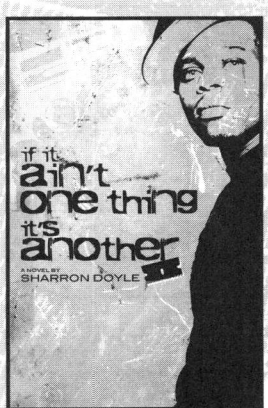

IF IT AIN'T ONE THING ITS ANOTHER
AUTHOR // **SHARRON DOYLE**
ISBN: 0975945316X // $14.95

SPOT RUSHERS
AUTHOR // **BRANDON McCALLA**
ISBN: 097594531 // $14.95

HUSTLE HARD
AUTHOR // **BLAINE MARTIN**
ISBN: 097594531 // $14.95

AugustusPublishing.com

AUGUSTUS PUBLISHING

ORDERFORM

Make All Checks Payable To: **Augustus Publishing** 33 Indian Road Ny, Ny 10034
Shipping Charges: Ground One Book $4.95 / Each Additional Book $1.00

Titles	Price	Qty	Total
Ghetto Girls (Special Edition) / Anthony Whyte ISBN: 0975945319	14.95		
Ghetto Girls Too / Anthony Whyte ISBN: 0975945300	14.95		
Ghetto Girls 3: Soo Hood / Anthony Whyte ISBN: 0975945351	14.95		
The Blue Circle / Keisha Seignious ISBN: 0975945335	14.95		
Booty Call *69 / Erick S Gray ISBN: 0975945343	14.95		
If It Ain't One Thing - It's Another / Sharron Doyle ISBN: 097594536X	14.95		
It Can Happen In A Minute / S.m. Johnson ISBN: 0975945378	14.95		
Woman's Cry: Llantó de la mujer / Vanessa Mártir ISBN: 0975945386	14.95		
A Good Day To Die / James Hendricks ISBN: 0975945327	14.95		
Lip Stick Diaries / Various Female Authors ISBN: 0975945394	14.95		
Spot Rushers / Brandon McCalla ISBN: 0979281628	14.95		
Hustle Hard / Blaine Martin ISBN: 0979281636	14.95		
	Subtotal		
	Shipping		
	8.625% Tax		
	Total		

Name
Company
Address
City   State   Zip
Phone   Fax
Email

Augustuspublishing.com / Info@augustuspublishing.com